"I'm sorry."

Belle shivered. She tugged away from his hold, that wasn't really a hold at all when Cage let go of her so easily, and she was grateful she hadn't betrayed the way he made her feel.

"I'm sorry, too," she whispered.

About so many things.

She walked out, leaving Cage standing there in the barn, surrounded by weights and mats and bars and bells, all procured with the intention of helping his daughter walk and run and dance again.

Just then, however, it felt to Belle as if she and Cage were the ones in need of walking lessons.

Dear Reader,

It's that time of year again—back to school! And even if you've left your classroom days far behind you, if you're like me, September brings with it the quest for everything new, especially books! We at Silhouette Special Edition are happy to fulfill that jones, beginning with *Home on the Ranch* by Allison Leigh, another in her bestselling MEN OF THE DOUBLE-C series. Though the Buchanans and the Days had been at odds for years, a single Buchanan rancher—Cage— would do anything to help his daughter learn to walk again, including hiring the only reliable physical therapist around. Even if her last name did happen to be Day....

Next, THE PARKS EMPIRE continues with Judy Duarte's *The Rich Man's Son,* in which a wealthy Parks scion, suffering from amnesia, winds up living the country life with a single mother and her baby boy. And a man passing through town notices more than the *passing* resemblance between himself and newly adopted infant of the local diner waitress, in *The Baby They Both Loved* by Nikki Benjamin. In *A Father's Sacrifice* by Karen Sandler, a man determined to do the right thing insists that the mother of his child marry him, and finds love in the bargain. And a woman's search for the truth about her late father leads her into the arms of a handsome cowboy determined to give her the life her dad had always wanted for her, in *A Texas Tale* by Judith Lyons. Last, a man with a new face revisits the ranch—and the woman—that used to be his. Only, the woman he'd always loved was no longer alone. Now she was accompanied by a five-year-old girl...with very familiar blue eyes....

Enjoy, and come back next month for six complex and satisfying romances, all from Silhouette Special Edition!

Gail Chasan
Senior Editor

Please address questions and book requests to:
Silhouette Reader Service
U.S.: 3010 Walden Ave., P.O. Box 1325, Buffalo, NY 14269
Canadian: P.O. Box 609, Fort Erie, Ont. L2A 5X3

ALLISON LEIGH

Home on the Ranch

SPECIAL EDITION®

Published by Silhouette Books

America's Publisher of Contemporary Romance

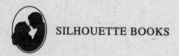 **SILHOUETTE BOOKS**

ISBN 0-373-24633-1

HOME ON THE RANCH

Copyright © 2004 by Allison Lee Davidson

All rights reserved. Except for use in any review, the reproduction or utilization of this work in whole or in part in any form by any electronic, mechanical or other means, now known or hereafter invented, including xerography, photocopying and recording, or in any information storage or retrieval system, is forbidden without the written permission of the editorial office, Silhouette Books, 233 Broadway, New York, NY 10279 U.S.A.

All characters in this book have no existence outside the imagination of the author and have no relation whatsoever to anyone bearing the same name or names. They are not even distantly inspired by any individual known or unknown to the author, and all incidents are pure invention.

This edition published by arrangement with Harlequin Books S.A.

® and TM are trademarks of Harlequin Books S.A., used under license. Trademarks indicated with ® are registered in the United States Patent and Trademark Office, the Canadian Trade Marks Office and in other countries.

Visit Silhouette Books at www.eHarlequin.com

Printed in U.S.A.

Books by Allison Leigh

Silhouette Special Edition

Stay... #1170
The Rancher and the Redhead #1212
A Wedding for Maggie #1241
A Child for Christmas #1290
Millionaire's Instant Baby #1312
Married to a Stranger #1336
Mother in a Moment #1367
Her Unforgettable Fiancé #1381
The Princess and the Duke #1465
Montana Lawman #1497
Hard Choices #1561
Secretly Married #1591
Home on the Ranch #1633

*Men of the Double-C Ranch

ALLISON LEIGH

started early by writing a Halloween play that her grade-school class performed. Since then, though her tastes have changed, her love for reading has not. And her writing appetite simply grows more voracious by the day.

She has been a finalist in the RITA® Award and the Holt Medallion contests. But the true highlights of her day as a writer are when she receives word from a reader that they laughed, cried or lost a night of sleep while reading one of her books.

Born in Southern California, Allison has lived in several different cities in four different states. She has been, at one time or another, a cosmetologist, a computer programmer and a secretary. She has recently begun writing full-time after spending nearly a decade as an administrative assistant for a busy neighborhood church, and currently makes her home in Arizona with her family. She loves to hear from her readers, who can write to her at P.O. Box 40772, Mcsa, AZ 85274-0772.

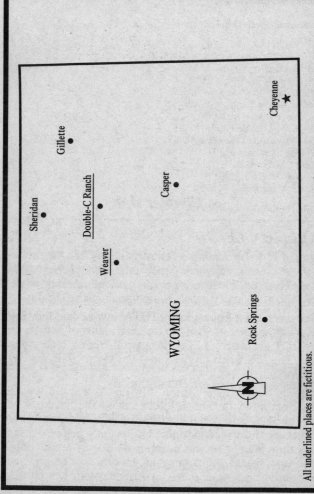

WYOMING

Sheridan

Gillette

Double-C Ranch

Weaver

Casper

Cheyenne

Rock Springs

N

All underlined places are fictitious.

Chapter One

"He is not an ogre."

Belle Day flicked her windshield wipers up to frenzied and tightened her grip around the steering wheel of her Jeep. She focused harder on the unfamiliar road, slowing even more to avoid the worst of the flooding, muddy ruts.

It wasn't the weather, or the road, or the unfamiliar drive that had her nerves in a noose, though. It was the person waiting at the end of the drive.

"He is *not* an ogre." Stupid talking to herself. She'd have to keep that to a minimum when she arrived. Not that she did it all the time.

Only when she was nervous.

Why had she agreed to this?

Her tire hit a dip her searching gaze had missed, and the vehicle rocked, the steering wheel jerking violently in her grip. She exhaled roughly and considered pulling over, but discarded the idea. The sooner she got to the Lazy-B, the sooner she could leave.

Not exactly positive thinking, Belle. Why are you doing this?

Her fingers tightened a little more on the wheel. "Lucy," she murmured. Because she wanted to help young Lucy Buchanan. Wanted to help her badly enough to put up with Lucy's father, Cage.

Who was not an ogre. Just because the therapist she was replacing had made enough complaints about her brief time here that they'd found a way through Weaver's grapevine didn't mean *her* experience would be similar.

That's not the only reason. She ignored the whispered thought. The road curved again, and she saw the hooked tree Cage had told her to watch for. Another quarter mile to go.

At least the ruts in the road were smoothing out and she stopped worrying so much about bouncing off into the ditch. The rain was still pouring down, though. Where the storm had come from after weeks of bone-dry weather, she had no idea. Maybe it had been specially ordered up to provide an auspicious beginning to her task.

She shook her head at the nonsense running through it, and slowed before the quarter-mile mark. It was raining and that was a good thing for a state that had been too dry for too long. She finally turned off the rutted road.

The gate that greeted her was firmly closed. She studied it for a moment, but of course the thing didn't magically open simply because she wished it.

She let out a long breath, pushed open the door and dashed into the rain. Her tennis shoes slid on the slick mud and she barely caught herself from landing on her butt. By the time she'd unhooked the wide, swinging gate, she was drenched. She drove through, then got out again and closed it. And then, because she couldn't possibly get *any* wetter unless she jumped in a river, she peered through the sheet of rain at Cage Buchanan's home.

It was hardly an impressive sight. Small. No frills. A porch ran across the front of the house, only partially softening the brick dwelling. But the place did look sturdy, as the rain sluiced from the roof, gushing out the gutter spouts.

She slicked back her hair and climbed into her Jeep once more to drive the rest of the way. She parked near the front of the house. Despite the weather, the door was open, but there was a wooden screen. She couldn't see much beyond it, though.

She grabbed her suitcase with one wet hand before shoving out of the Jeep, then darted up the narrow edge of porch steps not covered by a wheelchair ramp. A damp golden retriever sat up to greet her, thumping his tail a few times.

"You the guard dog?" Belle let the curious dog sniff her hand as she skimmed the soles of her shoes over the edge of one of the steps. The rain immediately turned the clumps of mud into brick-red rivulets that flowed down over the steps. Beneath the protection of the porch overhang, she wiped her face again, and flicked her hair behind her shoulders. Of all days not to put it in a ponytail. She couldn't have arrived looking more pathetic if she'd tried.

She knocked on the frame of the screen door, trying not to be obvious about peering inside and trying to pretend she wasn't shivering. Even sopping wet, she wasn't particularly cold. Which meant the shivers were mostly nerves and she hated that.

She knocked harder. The dog beside her gave a soft *woof*.

"Ms. Day!" A young, cheerful voice came from inside the door, then Belle saw Lucy wheel into view. "The door's open. Better leave Strudel outside, though."

"Strudel, huh?" Belle gave the dog a sympathetic pat. "Sorry, fella." She went inside, ignoring another rash of shivers that racked through her. It was a little harder to ignore Strudel's faint whine when she closed the screen on him, though.

She set her suitcase on the wood-planked floor, taking in the interior of the house with a quick glance. Old-fashioned furnishings dominated mostly by a fading cabbage rose print. An antique-looking upright piano sat against one wall, an older model TV against the other. The room was clean but not overly tidy, except for the complete lack of floor coverings. Not even a scatter rug to quiet the slow drip of water puddling around her.

She looked at the girl who was the reason for her waterlogged trek. "Your hair has grown." Too thin, she thought. And too pale. But Lucy's blue eyes sparkled and her golden hair gleamed.

Lucy dimpled and ran a hand down the braid that rested over her thin shoulder. "It's dry, too. Come on. We'll get you some towels." She turned her chair with practiced movements.

Belle quickly followed. Her tennis shoes gave out a wet squeak with each step. They were considerably louder than the soft turn of Lucy's wheelchair.

She glanced through to the kitchen when they passed it. Empty. More than a few dishes sat stacked in the white sink. The stove looked ancient but well preserved.

"This is my room." Lucy waved a hand as she turned her chair on a dime, stopping toward the end of the hall, unadorned except for a bookshelf weighted down with paperbacks. "Used to be Dad's, but we switched 'cause of the stairs." She smiled mischievously. "Now I have my own bathroom."

Belle's gaze drifted to the staircase. "And up there was your old room?"

"Yeah, but the bathroom's in the hall. Not the same. There's an empty room up there, though. You don't have to sleep, like, on the couch or nothing."

Belle smiled. "I know. Your dad told me I'd have my own room." She hoped the two upstairs rooms were at least at opposite ends of the hall.

She walked into Lucy's bedroom. It may have been temporarily assigned because of Lucy's situation, but it bore no sign that it had ever been anything but a twelve-year old girl's bedroom. There was pink… everywhere. Cage had even painted the walls pale pink. And in those rare places where there wasn't pink, there was purple. Shiny, glittery purple.

Hiding her thoughts, she winked cheerfully at Lucy and squished into the bathroom where the towels were—surprise, surprise—pink with purple stripes. As she bent over hurriedly scrubbing her hair between a towel to take the worst of the moisture out, she heard the roll of Lucy's chair. "Is your dad around?" She couldn't put off meeting with him forever, after all. He *was* employing her. He'd hired her to provide both the physical therapy his daughter needed following a horseback-riding accident several months ago, and the tutoring she needed to make up for the months of school she'd missed as a result.

Lucy didn't answer and she straightened, flinging the towel around her shoulders, turning. "Lucy? Oh."

Six plus feet of rangy muscle stood there, topped by sharply carved features, bronze hair that would be wavy if he let it grow beyond two inches and eyes so pale a blue they were vaguely heart stopping.

"I guess you are." She pushed her lips into a smile that, not surprisingly, Cage Buchanan didn't return. He'd hired her out of desperation, and they both knew it.

After all, he loathed the ground she walked.

"You drove out here in this weather."

Her smile stiffened even more. In fact, a sideways glance at the mirror over the sink told her the stretch of her lips didn't much qualify for even a stiff smile. "So it would seem." It was easier to look beyond him at Lucy, so that's what she did. "Sooner we get started, the better. Right Lucy?"

For the first time, Belle saw Lucy's expression darken. The girl's lips twisted and she looked away.

So, chalk one up for the efficiency of Weaver's grapevine again. Judging by the girl's expression, the rumor about Lucy's attitude toward her physical therapy was true.

Belle looked back at Cage. She knew he'd lived on

the Lazy-B his entire life. Had been running it, so the stories went, since he'd been in short pants.

Yet she could count their encounters in person on one hand.

None of the occasions had been remotely pleasant.

Belle had had her first personal encounter with Cage before Lucy's accident over the issue of Lucy going on a school field trip to Chicago. Lucy had been the only kid in her class who hadn't been allowed to go on the week-long trip. Belle—as the newest school employee—had been drafted into chaperone service and had foolishly thought she'd be able to talk Cage into changing his mind.

She'd been wrong. He'd accused her of being inter-fering and flatly told her to stay out of his business.

It had not been pleasant.

Had she learned her lesson, though? Had she given up the need to *somehow* give something back to his fam-ily? No.

Which only added to her tangle of feelings where Cage Buchanan was concerned. Feelings that had ex-isted long before she'd come to Weaver six months ago with great chunks of her life pretty much in tatters.

"Did you bring a suitcase?"

She nodded. "I, um, left it by the front door."

He inclined his head a few degrees and his gaze drifted impassively down her wet form. "I'll take it up-stairs for you."

"I can—" But he'd already turned on his heel, walk-ing away. Soundless, even though he was wearing scuffed cowboy boots with decidedly worn-down heels.

If she hadn't had a stepfamily full of men who

walked with the same soundless gait, she'd have spent endless time wondering how he could move so quietly.

She looked back at Lucy and smiled. A real one. She'd enjoyed Lucy from the day they'd met half a year ago in the P.E. class Belle had been substitute teaching. And she'd be darned if she'd let her feelings toward the sweet girl be tainted by the past. "So, that's a lot of ribbons and trophies on that shelf over there." She gestured at the far wall and headed toward it, skirting the pink canopied bed. "Looks like you've been collecting them for a lot of years. What are they all for?"

"State Fair. 4-H." Lucy rolled her chair closer.

Belle plucked one small gold trophy off the shelf. "And this one?"

"Last year's talent contest."

Belle ran her finger over the brass plate affixed to the trophy base. "First place. I'm not surprised." Belle had still been in Cheyenne then with no plans whatsoever about coming to Weaver for any reason other than to visit her family. Her plans back then had involved planning her wedding and obtaining some seniority at the clinic.

So much for that.

"Won't be in the contest this year, that's for sure."

"Because you're not dancing at the moment?" Belle set the trophy back in its place. "You could sing." She ignored Lucy's soft snort. "Or play piano. I thought I remembered you telling me once that you took lessons."

"I did."

"But not now?"

Lucy shrugged. Her shoulders were impossibly thin.

Everything about her screamed "delicate" but Belle knew the girl was made of pretty stern stuff.

"Yeah, I still take lessons. But it doesn't matter. If I can't dance then I don't want to be in the contest. It's stupid anyway. Just a bunch of schoolkids."

"I don't know about stupid," Belle countered easily. Most talented school kids from all over the state. "But we can focus on *next* year." She took the towel from her shoulders and folded it, then sat on top of it on the end of Lucy's bed. She leaned forward and touched the girl's knee. The wicked scar marring Lucy's skin was long and angry. "Don't look so down, kiddo. People can do amazing things when they really want. Remember, I've seen you in action. And I already think you're pretty amazing."

"Miss Day."

Belle jerked a little. Cage Buchanan was standing in the doorway again. She kept her smile in place, but it took some work. "You'd better start calling me Belle," she suggested, deliberately cheerful. "Both of you. Or I'm not going to realize you're talking to me."

"The students called you Miss Day during the school year," he countered smoothly.

"You're not a student, Cage." She pointedly used his name. More to prove that she could address the man directly than to disprove that whole ogre thing. The fact was, she knew he was deliberately focusing on her surname. And she knew why.

She was a Day. And he hated the Day family.

His eyes were impossible to read. Intensely blue but completely inscrutable. "I need a few minutes of your time. Then you can...settle in."

Belle hoped she imagined his hesitation before *set-*

tle. Despite everything, she wasn't prepared to be sent out on her ear before she'd even had a session with Lucy. For one thing, she really wanted to help the girl. For another, her ego hadn't exactly recovered from its last professional blow.

She was aware of Lucy watching her, a worried expression on her face. And she absolutely did *not* want to worry the girl. It wasn't Lucy's problem that she had a…slight…problem with the girl's dad. "Sure." She rose, taking the towel with her. "Then I'll change into something dry, and you—" she gently tugged the end of Lucy's braid "—and I can get started."

The girl's expression was hardly a symphony of excitement. But she did eventually nod, and Belle was happy for that.

She squeaked across the floor in her wet sneakers and, because Cage didn't look as if he would be moving anytime this century, she slipped past him into the hall. He was tall and he was broad and she absolutely did not touch him, yet she still tamped down hard on a shiver.

Darned nerves.

"Kitchen," he said.

Ogre, she thought, then mentally kicked herself. He was a victim of circumstances far more than she was. And he *had* painted his bedroom pink for Lucy, for heaven's sake. Was that the mark of an ogre?

She turned into the kitchen.

"Sit down."

There were three chairs around an old-fashioned table that—had it been in someone else's home— would have been delightfully retro. Here, it obviously was original, rather than a decorating statement. She sat down on one of the chairs and folded her hands together atop the table, waiting expectantly. If he wanted to send her home already, then he would just have to say so because *she* wasn't going to invite the words from him. She'd had enough of failure lately, thank you very much.

But in the game of staring, she realized all too quickly that he was a master. And she…was not.

So she bluffed. She lifted her eyebrows, doing the best imitation of her mother that she could summon, and said calmly, "Well?"

Interfering, Cage thought, eying her oval face. Interfering, annoyingly superior, and—even wet and bedraggled—too disturbing for his peace of mind.

But more than that, she'd managed to make him feel out of place. And Cage particularly didn't like that feeling.

But damned if that wasn't just the way he felt standing there in his own kitchen, looking at the skinny, wet woman sitting at the breakfast table where he'd grown up eating his mother's biscuits and sausage gravy. And it was nobody's fault but his own that Miss Belle Day— with her imperiously raised eyebrows and waist-length brown hair—was there at all.

He pulled out a chair, flipped it around and straddled it, then focused on the folder sitting on the table, rather than on Belle. This was about his daughter, and there wasn't much in this world he wouldn't do for Lucy. Including put up with a member of the Day family, who up until a few years ago had remained a comfortable distance away in Cheyenne.

If only she wasn't…disturbing. If only he hadn't felt that way from the day they'd met half a year ago.

Too many "if onlys." Particularly for a man who'd been baptized in the art of dealing with reality for more years than he could remember.

He flipped open the folder, reining in his thoughts. "Doctors' reports." He shoved a sheaf of papers toward her. "Notes from the last two PTs." Two different physical therapists. Two failures. He was running out of patience, which he'd already admitted to her two weeks ago when he'd flatly told her why the other two hadn't worked out; and he was definitely running out of money, which he had no intention of ever admitting to her.

He watched Belle's long fingers close over the papers as she drew them closer to read. He pinched the bridge of his nose before realizing he was even doing it. Maybe that's what came from having a headache for so many months now.

"Your last therapist—" Belle tilted her head, studying the writing, and a lock of tangled hair brushed the table, clinging wetly "—Annette Barrone. This was her schedule with Lucy?" She held up a report.

"Yeah."

She shook her head slightly and kept reading. "It's not a very aggressive plan."

"Lucy's only twelve."

Belle's gaze flicked up and met his, then flicked away. He wondered if she thought the same thing he'd thought. That Annette had been more interested in impressing her way into his bed than getting his daughter out of her wheelchair.

But she didn't comment on that. "Lucy's not an ordinary twelve-year-old, though," she murmured. The papers rustled in the silent kitchen as she turned one thin sheet to peruse the next. Her thumb tapped rhythmically against the corner of the folder.

"My daughter is not abnormal."

Her thumb paused. She looked up again. Her eyes, as rich a brown as the thick lashes that surrounded them, narrowed. "Of course she's not abnormal. I never suggested she was." She moistened her lips, then suddenly closed the folder and rested her slender forearms on top of it, leaning toward him across the table. "What I *am* saying is that Lucy is highly athletic. Her ballet dancing. Her riding. School sports. She is only twelve, yes. But she's still an athlete, and her therapy should reflect that, if there's to be any hope of a full recovery. That's what you want, right?" Her gaze never strayed from his.

He eyed her. "You're here."

She looked a little uneasy for a moment. "Right. Of course. You wouldn't keep hunting up therapists who are willing to come all the way out here to the Lazy-B on a lark. But my point is that you *could* just drive her into town for sessions a few times a week. She could even have her tutoring done in town. All of her teachers want to see her be able to start school again in the fall with her class, rather than falling behind." Her lips curved slightly. "The cost for the therapy would be considerably less if you went into town. You could have a therapist of your choice work with Lucy at the Weaver hospital. I know the place isn't entirely state of the art, but it's so new and the basics are there—"

"I'll worry about the cost." That faint smile of hers

died at his interruption. "You're supposed to be good at what you do. Are you?"

Her expression tightened. "I'm going to help Lucy."

It wasn't exactly an answer. But Cage cared about two things. Lucy and the Lazy-B. He was damned if he'd admit how close he was to losing both. Like it or not, he needed Belle Day.

And he hoped his father wasn't rolling over in his grave that this woman was temporarily living on the ranch that had been in the Buchanan family for generations.

He stood, unable to stand sitting there for another minute. "Set whatever schedule you need. Your stuff is in the room upstairs at the end of the hall. Get yourself dry. I've got work to do."

He ignored her parted lips—as if she was about to speak—and strode out of the room.

The sooner Belle did what he hired her for and went on her way, the better. They didn't have to like each other. The only thing he cared about was that she help Lucy and prove that he could provide the best for his daughter.

Once Belle Day had done that, she could take her skinny, sexy body and interfering ways and stay the hell out of his life.

Chapter Two

The rain continued the rest of the afternoon, finally slowing after dinner, which Belle and Lucy ate alone. Cage had shown his face briefly before then, but only to tell Lucy to heat up something from the fridge and not to wait on him. Belle had seen the shadow in Lucy's eyes at that, though the girl didn't give a hint to her father that she was disappointed. And it was that expression that kept haunting Belle later that evening after Lucy had gone to bed. Haunted her enough that she didn't close herself up in the guest room to avoid any chance encounter with Cage.

Instead, she hung around in the living room, knowing that sooner or later he would have to pass through the room in order to go upstairs. But, either she underestimated his intention to avoid her as much as possible, or he had enough bookkeeping to keep him busy for hours on end in his cramped little office beyond the stairs.

When she realized her nose was in danger of hitting the pages of the mystery she'd borrowed from the hallway shelf, she finally gave up and went upstairs. Walked past the bedroom that Cage had traded with his daughter. The door was open and she halted, took a step back, looking through the doorway. There was only the soft light from the hall to go by, but it was enough to see that the room was pink.

He hadn't painted over the walls in Lucy's original room as if she was never going to be able to return to it.

She chose to take that as a good sign. All too many people entered physical therapy without really believing they'd come out on the other side.

Though the room was pink, it still looked spare. All she could see from her vantage point was the bed with a dark-colored quilt tossed over the top, a dresser and a nightstand with a framed photograph sitting on it. The photo was angled toward the bed.

"Something interesting in there?"

She jerked and looked back to see Cage stepping up onto the landing. He looked as tired as she felt. "Pink," she said, feeling foolish.

His long fingers closed over the newel post at the head of the stairs. He had a ragged-looking bandage covering the tip of his index finger. She'd noticed it earlier. Had squelched the suggestion that she rewrap it for him, knowing it wouldn't be welcomed.

His eyebrows pulled together. "What?"

She gestured vaguely. "The walls. They're pink. I was just noticing that, I mean."

"Luce likes pink." His lashes hid his expression. "She's a girl."

"My sister likes pink." Belle winced inwardly. What an inane conversation.

"And you?"

"And I...what?" He probably thought she was an idiot.

"Don't like pink?"

"No. No, pink is fine. But I'm more of a, um, a red girl."

His lips lifted humorlessly. "Pink before it's diluted. You fixed pizza."

She blinked a little at the abrupt shift. "Veggie pizza. There's some left in the refrigerator."

"I know. And I'm not paying you to play cook."

That derailed her for half a moment. But she rallied quickly. Anyone with two eyes in their head could see the Buchanans could use a helping hand. "I didn't mind and Lucy—"

"I mind."

She stiffened. Did he expect her to assure him it wouldn't happen again? "The whole wheat pizza and fresh vegetables, the fact that Lucy didn't want to eat that leftover roast beef you told her to eat, or the fact that *I* dared to use your kitchen? Any other rules I need to know about?"

Apparently, he didn't recognize that her facetious comment required no answer. "Stay away from the stables."

"Afraid a *Day* might hurt the horses? Why did you even bother talking me into taking this job?"

"The horse that threw Lucy is in the stable. I don't want her tempted to go there, and if you do, she'll want to, as well. And the only thing my daughter needs from you is your expertise."

"Which, by your tone, it would seem you doubt I possess. Again, it makes me wonder why you came to me, not once but twice, to get me to take on Lucy's case for the summer." The hallway seemed to be shrinking. Or maybe it was her irritation taking up more space as it grew.

"You have the right credentials."

"Just the wrong pedigree." Her flat statement hovered in the air between them.

Every angle of his sharp features tightened. "Is your room comfortable enough?"

"It's fine." She eyed him and wondered how a man she barely knew could be so intertwined in her life. "Sooner or later we might as well talk about it." His expression didn't change and she exhaled. "Cage, what happened was tragic, but it was a long time ago." She ought to know.

Finally, some life entered his flinty features, and his expression was so abruptly, fiercely alive that she actually took a step back, earning a bump of her elbow against the wall behind her.

"A *long* time ago?" His bronze hair seemed to ripple along with the coldness in his voice as he towered over her. "I'll mention that to my mother next time I visit her. Of course, she probably won't mind, since she barely remembers one day to the next."

Belle's stomach clenched. Not with fear, but sympathy and guilt. And she knew he'd never in a million years accept those sentiments from her, if he even believed she was capable of experiencing it.

She'd heard he was overbearing. But he believed she was the daughter of a devil.

She folded her hands together. Well, she'd been warned, hadn't she? "This was a bad idea. I shouldn't have come here. You…you should bring Lucy into Weaver. I will work with her there." She didn't officially have hospital privileges, but she had a few connections who could help arrange it, namely her stepsister-in-law, Dr. Rebecca Clay. And it didn't matter *where* Belle and Lucy did the tutoring.

"I want you here. I've told you that."

Belle pushed her fingers through her hair, raking it back from her face. "But, Cage. It just doesn't make any sense. Yes, I know it's a long drive to make every few days into town, but—"

His teeth flashed in a barely controlled grimace. "My daughter will have the best care there is. If that seems extravagant to you, I don't care. Now, are we going to have this—" he barely hesitated "—discussion every time we turn around? Because I'd prefer to see something more productive out of your presence here. God knows I'm paying you enough."

She sank her teeth into her tongue to keep from telling him what he could do with that particular compensation. Compensation they both knew was considerably less than she could have charged. "I'd like my time to be productive, too," she said honestly. "I have no desire to spend unnecessary time under your roof."

"Well, there's something we agree on, then."

Her fingers were curled so tightly against her palms that even her short nails were causing pain. "And here's something else we'd better agree on." She kept her voice low, in deference to Lucy sleeping downstairs. "Lucy doesn't need the added stress of knowing you detest me, so maybe you could work on summoning a little…well, *friendliness* is probably asking too much. But if Lucy senses that you don't trust me to do my best with her, then she's not going to, either, no matter *how* well she and I got along when she was in my P.E. class."

"I don't need you telling me what my daughter needs. I've been her only parent since she was born."

"And it's amazing that she's turned out as well as she has." She winced at the unkind words. "I'm sorry. That was—"

"True enough." He didn't look particularly offended. "She *is* amazing."

Belle nibbled the inside of her lip as thick silence settled over them. Should she have listened to her mother's warning that she was getting in over her head? Not because of the skill she would require to work with Lucy—as her therapist as well as a tutor—but because of who Lucy *was?*

Probably.

She sighed a little and pressed her palms together. "Lucy is a great kid, Cage. And I really do want to help her." That was the whole point of all this.

Mostly.

A muscle flexed in his jaw and his gaze slid sideways, as if he was trying to see the bedroom downstairs where his daughter slept. "If I believed you didn't, you wouldn't be here."

Which, apparently, was as much a concession as she was likely to get out of the man. For now, anyway. For-

tunately, somewhere in her life she'd learned that a retreat didn't always signify defeat.

"Well. I guess I'll hit the sack." She was twenty-
seven years old, but she still felt her face heat at the
words. As if the man didn't know she'd be climbing into
bed under his roof. She was such a head case. Better to
focus on *the job*. The last time he'd come to her house—
after she'd already refused Lucy's case once—he'd admitted that he'd fired Annette Barrone because of her
overactive hormones. Belle had assured him that he had
no worries from her on *that* score.

As if.

"I went over and checked out the barn earlier," she
said evenly when neither one of them moved. "The
setup is remarkable." And another indication of his devotion to his daughter. Every piece of equipment that
she could have wished for had been there, and then
some. The hospital in town should only be so lucky. "I
rearranged things a little. If that's all right."

Now, his hooded gaze slid back over her face. And
she refused to acknowledge that the shiver creeping up
her spine had anything to do with his intensely blue
gaze.

"Use your judgment."

She nodded. "Okay, then." The door to her bedroom
was within arm's reach. Not at *all* at opposite ends of the
hall from his. "Good night." She wished he would turn into
his own bedroom. But he just stood there. And feeling id-
iotic, she unplastered her back from the wall behind her
and went through the door, quickly shutting it behind her.

A moment later, she heard the squeak of a floor-
board, and the close of another door.

Relief sagged through her. After changing into her pajamas, she crossed to the bed and sat on it, dragging her leather backpack-style purse up beside her. She rummaged through it until she found her cell phone and quickly dialed.

A moment later, her sister, Nikki, answered with no ceremony. "So, are you there?".

Belle propped the pillow behind her and scooted back against it. The iron-frame bed squeaked softly, as if to remind her that it had survived years and years of use. It was a vaguely comforting sound. "Yes." She kept her voice low. The house might be sturdy, but the walls were thin enough that she could hear the rush of the shower from the bathroom across the hall.

She stared hard at the log-cabin pattern of the quilt beneath her until the image *that* thought brought about faded. "The drive was hellacious in the rain."

"Well, we've heard Squire say often enough that Cage Buchanan doesn't like visitors, so there's not a lot of need for him to make sure the road is easy."

"I know." Squire Clay was their stepfather, having married their mother several years earlier. She tugged at her ear. "Anyway, I know it's late. You were probably already in bed."

"It's okay. I wouldn't have slept until I knew you hadn't been beheaded at the guy's front door."

"He's not *that* bad."

"Not bad to look at, maybe. I still can't believe you took this job. What do you hope to prove, anyway?"

"Nothing," Belle insisted. "It's just a job to fill the summer until—" *if* "—I come back to the clinic."

Nikki snorted softly. "Maybe. But I'm betting you

think this is your last chance to prove to yourself that you're not a failure."

Belle winced. "Don't be ridiculous, Nik."

"Come on, Belle. What other reason would have finally made you agree to that man's request?"

"*That man* has a name."

Nikki's sudden silence was telling. That was the problem with having a twin. But Belle was not going to get into some deep discussion over her motivation in taking on this particular job. "Speaking of the clinic," she said deliberately. "How are things there?"

"Fine."

Now it was Belle's turn to remain silent.

"They still haven't hired anyone to replace you, if that's what you're worried about," Nikki finally said after a breathy huff.

"That's something, at least." And a bit of a minor miracle, given the number of patients the prestigious clinic handled. She still wasn't entirely sure it wasn't because of the position her sister held as administrative assistant to the boss that Belle had been put on a leave of absence rather than being dismissed.

"And I know you're wondering but won't ask," Nikki went on. "So I'll just tell you. Scott's only coming in once a week now."

She wasn't sure how she felt at the mention of him. A patient she hadn't managed to completely rehabilitate. Briefly a fiancé she shouldn't have completely trusted. "You've seen him?"

"Are you kidding? I hide out in my office. If I saw Scott Langtree in person, I'd be liable to kick him." Nikki paused for a moment and when she spoke, her voice was acid. "*She* comes with him, now, apparently. Has most of the staff in a snit because she's so arrogant. Not that I'm condoning what Scott did, but from what people around here are saying about his wife, it's no wonder the man was on the prowl for someone else."

Belle plucked at the point of a quilted star. "But you haven't seen her?"

"Nope. And I consider that a good thing. I'd have something to say to her, too, and then *I'd* have my tail in a sling at work, just like you."

Belle smiled faintly. Nikki was her champion and always had been. "Hardly like me. You'd never be stupid enough to fall for a guy who already had a wife."

"And you wouldn't have fallen for Scott, either, if he hadn't lied about being married," Nikki said after a moment. "Good grief, Belle. The man proposed to you and everything. It's not your fault that he left out the rather significant detail that he wasn't free to walk another aisle."

"I caused a scandal there."

"Scott created the scandal," Nikki countered rapidly, "and it was half a year ago, yet you're still punishing yourself."

Belle wanted to deny it, but couldn't. Her relationship with Scott Langtree *had* caused a scandal. One large enough to create the urgent need for Belle to take a leave of absence until the furor died down. But it wasn't even the scandal that weighed on Belle so much as the things Scott had told her in the end.

Things she didn't want to dwell on. Things like being a failure on every front. Personal. Professional. Things that a secret part of her feared could be true.

"So," she sat up a little straighter, determined. "Other than…that…how are things going at work? Did you get that raise you wanted?"

"Um. No. Not yet."

"Did you *ask* for it?"

"No. But—"

"But nothing. Nik, you stand up for me all the time. You've got to stand up for yourself, too. Alex would be lost without you, and it's high time he started realizing it. I swear, it would serve the man right if *you* quit." But she knew Nikki wasn't likely to do that. Alexander Reed ran the Huffington Sports Clinic, including its various locations around the country. He had degrees up the whazoo, and was a business marvel, according to Nikki.

Belle just found the man intimidating as all get-out, but had still worked her tail off to get a position there.

A position she *was* going back to, she assured herself inwardly.

"So, what's he like? Cage, I mean. As ornery as everyone says?"

Belle accepted Nikki's abrupt change of topic. Alex was too sensitive a subject for her sister to discuss for long. "He is not an ogre," she recited softly.

Nikki laughed a little. "Keep telling yourself that, Annabelle."

Belle smiled. "It's late. Get some sleep. I'll talk to you later."

"Watch your back," Nikki said, and hung up.

Belle thumbed off her phone and set it on the nightstand. She didn't need to watch her back where Cage Buchanan was concerned. But that didn't mean she would be foolish enough to let down her guard, either.

The bed squeaked again when she lay down and yanked the quilt up over her. Even though the day hadn't been filled with much physical activity, she was exhausted. But as soon as her head hit the pillow, her eyes simply refused to shut, and she lay there long into the night, puzzling over the man who slept on the other side of the bedroom wall.

When he heard the soft creak of bedsprings for the hundredth time, Cage tossed aside the book he was reading and glared at the wall between the two bedrooms. Even sleeping, the woman was an irritant, and as soon as she was busy for the day, he was going to oil her bedsprings.

The last thing he needed night after night was to hear the sound of that woman's slightest movement in the bed that was so old it had been ancient even when he'd used it as a kid.

He hadn't noticed the squeaks before. Not with either therapist. Hattie McDonald with her militant aversion to smiles and her equally strong dislike for the remoteness of his ranch, nor Annette Barrone who'd made it clear she'd rather be sleeping in his room, anyway.

He climbed out of bed—fortunately a newer model than the one next door—and pulled on his jeans. He'd never been prone to sleeplessness until six months ago when he'd gotten the first letter from Lucy's mother. A helluva way to kick off the New Year. She wanted to see her daughter, she'd claimed. A daughter she'd never even wanted to have in the first place. He'd put her off, not believing her threat that she'd enlist her parents if he didn't comply. When he'd known Sandi, she'd wanted nothing to do with her parents beyond spending her tidy trust fund in any manner sure to earn their dismay.

Only she hadn't been bluffing. And it was a lot harder to ignore the demand for access to Lucy when it came from Sandi's parents. Particularly when it was backed up by their family attorneys.

Then came Lucy's accident several weeks later and his insomnia had only gotten worse. In the past week, with Belle Day's arrival pending, it was a rare night if he got more than an hour or two of sleep at a stretch. It was pretty damn frustrating.

He'd given up coffee, counted sheep and even drunk some god-awful tea that Emmy Johannson—one of the few people he tolerated in Weaver—had suggested. Nothing had worked.

And now he could add Belle Day's bed-creaking presence to his nightly irritations.

Barefoot, he left his bedroom. He could no more not glare at her closed door than he could get a full night's sleep these days.

He went downstairs, automatically stepping around the treads that had their own squeak, and looked in on Lucy. She'd kicked off her blankets again and he went inside, carefully smoothing them back in place. She sighed and turned on her side, tucking her hands together beneath her cheek in the same way she'd done since she was only months old.

There were times it seemed like twelve minutes hadn't passed since then, much less twelve years. Yet here she was, on the eve of becoming a teenager.

That was the problem with baby girls.

They grew up and started thinking they weren't their dad's baby girl anymore.

He left her room, leaving the door ajar so he could hear if she cried out in her sleep. Since she'd been thrown off that damn horse he should have sent back to her grandparents the day it arrived, she'd been plagued in her sleep almost as much as Cage.

He didn't need any light to guide him as he went through the house. The place was as familiar to him as his own face. Nearly the only thing that had changed since his childhood was the bed he'd just left behind and, if he'd had any foresight of the financial hit he would soon be taking with all manner of legal and medical costs, he wouldn't have bought the thing last year at all.

He went out on the front porch where the air still carried the damp from the rain even though it had finally ceased. It was more than a little chilly, but he barely noticed as he sat down on the oversize rocking chair his mother had once loved.

If the room at the care center would have had space for it, he'd have moved it there for her years ago. There wasn't much she hadn't done sitting in the chair here on this very porch. She'd shelled peas, knitted sweaters and argued good-naturedly with Cage's father when he and Cage came in after a long day.

But her room, while comfortable enough, wasn't that spacious.

And the one time he'd brought her back to the Lazy-B, she hadn't remembered the chair any more than she remembered him.

He leaned back, propping his feet on the rail, and stared out into the darkness. Strudel soon appeared beside him, apparently forgiving Cage for his banishment after dining on yet another pair of Cage's boots. He scratched the dog's head for a minute, then Strudel heaved a sigh and flopped down on the porch. In seconds, the rambunctious pup was snoring.

Lucky dog.

There were a lot of things Cage wished for in his life. But right then, the thing at the top of the list was sleep. He'd nearly achieved it when he heard a short, sharp scream.

Lucy.

He bolted out of the chair, leaving it rocking crazily behind him as he went inside. And he slammed right into the slender body hurtling around the staircase.

He caught Belle's shoulders, keeping her from flying five feet backward from the impact. "Lucy—" Her voice was breathless. Probably because he'd knocked the wind clean out of her.

"She sometimes has nightmares since the accident." He realized his fingers were still pressing into her taut flesh and abruptly let go. His eyes, accustomed to the darkness, picked up the pale oval of her face, the faint sheen of her skin. A lot of skin, it seemed. She was wearing loose shorts and some strappy little top that betrayed the fact she wasn't skinny everywhere.

He deliberately stepped around her and went into Lucy's room. But his daughter was already quiet again. Still sleeping, as if nothing had disturbed her at all.

He raked his fingers through his hair, pressed the heels of his palms to his eyes. God, he was tired. Then he felt a light touch on his back and nearly jumped out of his skin. He turned, pulling Lucy's door nearly closed again. "What?"

His harsh whisper sent Belle backward almost as surely as their collision had.

"Sorry." Her voice was hushed. "I thought…" He felt her shrug more than saw it. "Nothing."

He pinched the bridge of his nose. He could smell her, rainwater fresh. The sooner she went back to bed, the better. He wasn't interested in what she thought. Or how she smelled. Or why she couldn't keep still for five minutes straight in that old bed. "You thought what?" he asked wearily. He wished the moon were shining a little less brightly through the picture window in the living room, because with each passing second, he could see her even more clearly. Definitely not *all* skinny.

She tugged up the narrow strap of her pajama top and hugged her arms to herself. "Nothing. It doesn't matter."

"Fine. Then go to bed."

She laughed—little more than a breath. "You sound like my dad used to."

He knew it was an innocent enough comment, aimed at the order he'd automatically given. Knowing it, though, didn't keep him from reacting. Before he could say something that might send her straight for the decrepit Jeep she'd arrived in—and away from any possibility of helping his daughter—he stepped around her and headed upstairs.

"Cage—"

He didn't want to hear anything she had to say. She'd said the magic word, sure to remind him just who she was, and to what lengths he'd been driven for his daughter's sake.

Dad.

"Just go to bed, Belle," he said, without looking back.

Chapter Three

Belle propped her hands on her hips and counted off a slow inhale and an even slower exhale. It was far too beautiful a morning, all promising with the golden sunrise, to let annoyance ruin it already. "Cage, I need to go over a few things with you about Lucy. I wanted to last night, but we never got to it."

His long legs barely paused as he passed her in the kitchen and headed out the back door of the house. "I've got a water tank that needs fixing." His tone was abrupt, as if he begrudged providing even that small bit of information.

Clearly, that somewhat approachable man she'd encountered in the middle of the night was banished again.

She hurried after him, letting the screen door slap shut noisily after her. She darted down the brick steps and jogged to keep up with him. She raised her voice.

"Lucy told me yesterday that you haven't worked with her on any of the exercises she's supposed to do on her own."

He stopped short. Tilted his head back for a moment, then slowly turned to face her. The shadow cast by his dark brown cowboy hat guarded the expression in his blue eyes, but even across the yards, she could feel the man's impatience. "I can't be in two places at once, Miss Day."

She mentally stiffened her spine at his exaggerated patience. So much for his one slip of calling her Belle the night before. "I'm aware of that, *Cage.* But you hired me to help Lucy, and—"

"I didn't hire you to lecture me on my ability to parent my own daughter."

Her lips parted. "I wasn't suggesting—"

His eyebrow rose, making him look even more sardonic than usual. "Weren't you?"

"No!"

"You weren't so reticent before Lucy's accident when you accused me of being unreasonable where she's concerned 'cause I wouldn't let her go on that godforsaken field trip to Chicago."

She glanced back at the house where Lucy still slept. The truth was, she *had* thought he was being unreasonable. But that was half a year ago and there were more important things on the agenda than eliciting his approval for a simple school field trip. "Look, maybe we should just talk about…things." She'd thought so all along, but hadn't had the courage to do so. Hadn't had much of an opportunity, either, given their brief conversations about Lucy where Cage had firmly kept control.

His expression hadn't changed. "You're here for one

reason only, Miss Day. It'd be better all around if you'd remember it."

Her jaw tightened uncomfortably. "I'm not the enemy, all right?"

His expression went from impatient to stony.

Her hands fell back to her sides. "I see. I *am* the enemy." Of course. Resulting from long-past history neither could change.

"If you need something that strictly pertains to Lucy—whether it's her therapy or her schoolwork—I have no doubt you'll let me know. Other than that—"

"—stay out of your hair?" Her tone was acid.

"That's one way to put it." He slapped the leather gloves he held against his palm. "Excuse me." He turned on his heel and strode away.

Belle stuck her tongue out at his back, and returned to the house. She yanked open the aging avocado-green refrigerator door. Maybe it was wrong of her, but she took great delight in making breakfast out of a leftover slice of pizza.

For Lucy, however, she set out an assortment of supplements on the counter, and then prepared a real breakfast. After peeking in the girl's bedroom to see that she was still sleeping, Belle pushed her feet into her running shoes and went back outside.

Even though the sky was clear, the dawn air still felt moist from the previous day, as she set off in a slow jog. Well beyond the simple brick house stood the sizable barn, doors open. She didn't want to wonder if Cage was in there. She wondered anyway, quickening her pace and then had to tell herself that she was being a ninny. The man ran a ranch. If he was in his barn, so what? Better there than in the house, bugging her and Lucy. Might present a problem when she and Lucy went to the barn to use the equipment, though.

She didn't doubt that he wanted the best for Lucy, which she certainly couldn't fault. Nevertheless, she'd never met a more antisocial man in her life. But, then, she'd been warned well enough before she took on this job, so complaining about it now was only so much wasted energy.

She figured she'd run a good hour by the time she returned to the house. She darted up the brick steps and went in through the front door, peeling out of her sweatshirt as she went. Surely the bathroom wouldn't still hold the lingering scent of Cage's soap by now.

The bathroom was no longer steamy, true. But she still took the fastest shower in her life before changing into fresh workout clothes. Then she went and woke Lucy. While the girl was dressing—something she didn't need assistance for—Belle wandered around the cozy living room.

She peered again at the silver-framed black-and-white photos hanging above the fireplace mantel. Cage's parents. And a young Cage. She sighed faintly as she studied the Buchanan family. She knew only too well that he'd been a teenager when he'd lost his father, and for all intents, his mother, as well. She ran her fingernail lightly over the image of the solemn-looking little boy. Were there any photos of him smiling?

Did Cage Buchanan ever smile? Ever laugh?

"Hey, Belle. I'm fixing waffles for breakfast. You know the fruity kind with whipped cream? Those frozen waffles are really good that way. Like dessert."

Belle looked back to see Lucy rolling her chair into the kitchen. She headed after her, and hid a smile at Lucy's disgruntled "Oh." Obviously, she'd seen the breakfast that Belle had already set out for her. There would be *no* frozen waffles.

She stepped around Lucy's narrow chair, tugging lightly on her gilded braid along the way. "It'll be good, I promise."

"Dad calls breakfasts like this 'sticks and weeds.'"

At that, Belle laughed softly. "Well, these sticks and weeds are a lot better for you than just a frozen waffle out of a box. It's a bran mix. And the strawberries on top are plenty sweet already without adding cream or sugar. But I could fix you eggs if you'd rather." She refused to wonder what Cage had eaten.

Lucy's perfectly shaped nose wrinkled. "Eggs. Gross."

"Yeah," Belle agreed. "I used to think so, too. But they're good for you, and there are lots of ways to fix them. So, what'll it be?"

Lucy eyed the table for a moment. Then she shrugged, and started to wheel forward. Belle casually stepped in her path and held out her hands expectantly.

And she waited.

And waited.

Finally, Lucy put her hands in Belle's. And she stood, her weight fully concentrated on her uninjured leg.

Belle winked cheerfully. Lucy wasn't the first patient she'd ever had, and certainly not the first who was leery of leaving the safety net, no matter how much they wanted to. But there was absolutely no reason why Lucy should still be depending entirely on the chair. "Stiff?"

Lucy nodded. There was a white line around her tight lips. Belle supported her as she twisted around and sat at the table. Then she tucked the wheelchair out of the way and sat down across from Lucy.

"Aren't you having any twigs?"

"Ate earlier. Not everyone sleeps in until noon."

Lucy rolled her eyes. "Yeah, right." She picked up the spoon and jabbed at her food. Gave an experimental taste. When the girl gave a surprised "hmm" and took another taste, Belle busied herself by filling a few water bottles and putting away the dishes they'd used and washed the night before as well as the stack that had already been there. She refused to feel guilty about it, either. It wasn't as if she was stealing the Buchanan family silver. She was just washing some crockery.

Lucy was nearly finished with her breakfast before she spoke again. "Did you see my dad this morning?"

"Yes, for a few minutes." Belle folded the dish towel and left it on the counter next to the sink. "He was heading out to fix a water tank."

"Oh." Lucy passed over her dishes.

Belle took them and set them in the sink. She flipped on the faucet to rinse them and glanced at Lucy. "Were you hoping for something different?"

Lucy shrugged but couldn't quite hide her diffidence. "He works the Lazy-B mostly by himself, you know."

Belle did know. She also knew that he hired on hands as needed, and that he usually didn't much want to admit to needing anything.

The man gave *loner* new meaning.

"I know." She smiled gently and moved the chair

back around for Lucy. "Come on. It's beautiful outside. Let's go for a little walk."

"No exercises yet?"

Lucy looked so hopeful that Belle had to smile as she helped the girl back into her chair. She crouched in front of her. "I'll tell you a secret," she confided lightly. "Exercise comes in all sorts of forms. Sometimes you don't even know you're doing it." She grazed her fingertips over Lucy's injured leg. "So. What do you say? A walk?"

Lucy nodded. Satisfied, Belle rose and handed Lucy a bottle of water, took one for herself and they headed out the front of the house, where Lucy's ramp was located.

Before long, Belle had to push the chair for Lucy because of the soft ground. The morning was delightfully quiet, broken only by the song of birds flirting in the tall cottonwoods that circled the house.

They walked all the way down the road to the gate then headed back again. "Do you like living on a ranch?"

Lucy lifted her shoulder, her fingers trailing up and down her braid. "It's okay, I guess. I used to spend part of the week in town. During the school year. Dad pays my friend Anya Johannson's mom for my board for part of the week. She teaches me piano and takes me to my dance lessons after school and stuff. Well, that's what we used to do." She tossed her braid behind her back.

They were within sight of the large red barn before Lucy spoke again. "You grew up in Cheyenne. Right?"

"Yup. Until I took the job at your school last year,

and when I went away to school, I'd always lived in Cheyenne. My sister, Nikki, still does. And my mother's been living at the Double-C Ranch since she married Squire Clay a while back."

"Were your parents divorced?"

"No. My dad died just before Nikki and I turned sixteen."

"Does she look like you? Nikki?"

Belle grinned. "Nah. She's the pretty one. Likes to shop for real clothes, not just jeans and workout gear. She looks like our mom. Auburn hair, an actual *figure*."

Lucy made a face, looking down at herself. She plucked the loose fabric of her pink T-shirt. "Yeah, well, I'm never gonna get…you know…boobs, either." Lucy's pale cheeks turned red. "Not that you don't, uh—"

Belle laughed. "It's okay. I do. But believe me, my sister got the larger helping in the chest department. And you're only twelve. You've got oodles of time yet."

"I'm gonna be thirteen next month."

Belle renewed her grasp on the handles of the chair, pushing it harder over the gravel road. "Why sound so glum about it? Are you going to have a party?"

"And do what?" Lucy thumped her hands on her chair.

"Who needs to *do* anything? You're going to be thirteen. I remember when Nik and I turned thirteen. We sat around with our friends and talked boys and makeup and music, and ate pizza and popcorn and had a blast."

"Doesn't matter. Dad's not going to let me have a party, anyway."

"Has he said that?" She would be upbeat if it killed her. "It never hurts to just ask. What's the worst that could happen? That he'd say no? You've already decided that, anyway. And he might surprise you." Whatever she'd seen or heard about Cage, the man was admittedly doing back flips for his daughter. What was one small party?

"He doesn't want me to do anything," Lucy insisted flatly. "Ever since my accident, he's been—" she shook her head, and fell silent.

"Worried about you, perhaps?" Belle maneuvered Lucy's chair through the opened barn door.

Lucy didn't respond to that. But she did respond to the changes Belle had made inside the barn. Most particularly the portable sound system she immediately flicked on. Banging music sounded out and Belle looked past Lucy's slack jaw as she handed her a sizable stack of CDs. "Hope there's something you like in there. I brought a little of everything."

Lucy flipped through the cases. Pulled one out. "Dad would like this."

Belle glanced over. Beatles. Drat. Her own personal favorite. "Anything *you* like?"

"Classics." Lucy shrugged diffidently. "Weird, huh?"

She felt as if she'd hit a treasure chest when she leaned over to flip down several more CDs in Lucy's lap and the girl laughed delightedly. "Beethoven. Pachelbel. Rachmaninoff. A little of everything."

Belle took the stack and set it on a crate next to the portable boom box. She slid in a CD and the strains of Mozart soared right up to the rafters.

Cage could hear the music a mile away. It was loud enough to scare his prized heifers out of breeding for another two seasons, and certainly loud enough to put his daughter in hearing aids before her next birthday. He wanted to race hell-bent for leather to the barn the way Strudel was, but he kept his pace even for Rory's sake. He was walking the horse back to the stable, hoping Rory's lame leg wouldn't require more than some TLC and rest. He knew the vet would come if he called, but it sat wrong in Cage's belly to keep looking at the balance of his bill with the man, knowing he wouldn't have it paid off anytime soon.

Naturally, the music grew even louder the closer he got to the barn and it showed no sign of abating even after he'd tended to Rory. He strode inside, only to stop short at the sight of Belle and Lucy. His daughter was lying on the incline bench. Not an unusual sight. But she was laughing, her head thrown back, blond hair streaming down her thin back, her face wreathed in smiles.

And Belle was laughing, too. She sat on the floor in front of the bench, her legs stretched into a position he thought only Olympic gymnasts could obtain, and she was leaning forward so far her torso was nearly resting on the blue mat beneath her. The position drew the tight black shirt she wore well above her waist, and for way too long, he couldn't look away from that stretch of lithe, feminine muscle.

Neither his daughter nor Belle noticed him and he felt like an outsider all over again. He liked it no more now than he had the previous day.

Then Belle turned her head, resting her cheek on the mat, and looked at him.

Not so unaware, after all.

"Come on in," she said. And even though she hadn't lifted her voice above the music, he still heard her. Her brown gaze was soft. Open.

She didn't even flinch when Strudel bounded over to her, snuffling at her face before hastily jumping over her to gleefully greet Lucy.

Safer to look at the slice of Belle's ivory back that showed below the shirt than those dark eyes. Maybe.

He deliberately strode to the boom box and turned down the volume. "Trying to make yourselves deaf?"

Lucy rolled her eyes. "It wasn't *that* loud."

He wished for the days when she hadn't yet learned to roll her eyes at him. "I'm going in to get your lunch."

"Belle already did."

At Lucy's blithe statement, Belle pushed herself up and drew her legs together, wriggling her red-painted toes. He saw a glint on one toe. She wore a toe ring. Figures.

"We left a plate for you," she said, apparently trusting that he wouldn't lecture her about her "place" in front of Lucy.

In that, she was correct. For now, at least. He eyed her for a moment. "Then I'll go down to get the mail."

Lucy ignored him as she flopped back on the slanted bench. Belle's gaze went from him to Lucy and back again. "If you have some time this afternoon, maybe Lucy could show you a few of the new exercises we've been working on."

He nodded and resettled his hat as he left. In the seconds before someone—his daughter probably—turned up the volume of the music again, he heard Lucy's flat statement. "He won't show. He never does."

It was an exaggeration, but that didn't stop the words from cutting. But he was only one man. As he'd told Belle, he couldn't do it all. Keep the Lazy-B going and spend hours with his daughter when he'd already hired a therapist for her for that very purpose. He whistled sharply and Strudel scrambled out of the barn, racing after him. The dog might have promise, after all.

He drove the truck down to get the mail. There was a cluster of boxes belonging to the half-dozen folks living out his direction. His place was the farthest out, though. The box was five miles from the house. Usually, he swung by on Rory. Not today.

Back in the house, he dumped the mail and the morning paper on the kitchen table and yanked open the refrigerator door. Sure enough. A foil-wrapped plate sat inside. The woman made pizza with whole wheat. Whole wheat? He wasn't even aware that he'd had any in his house. Either she'd brought it in her suitcase, which was entirely possible since she had no qualms about thinking she knew best where his family was concerned, or the stuff had been lurking in his cupboards courtesy of Emmy Johannson, who periodically brought groceries out for him.

God only knew what lurked on that plate under the foil. He ignored it and made himself a roast-beef sandwich, instead. He was standing at the counter eating it when he saw Belle through the window over the sink striding up to the rear of the house. He turned a page of the newspaper and continued reading. Something about a chili cook-off.

It wasn't engrossing stuff, but it was better than watching Belle. The woman had a way of moving and it was just better off, all around, if he didn't look too close. He didn't like her, or her family, and she was there only out of his own desperation. So he needed to get over the fact that she turned him on and he needed to do it yesterday.

The screen rattled as Belle pulled it open and popped into the kitchen. His gaze slid sideways to her feet. Scuffed white tennis shoes—a different pair than the wet blue ones the day before—now hid the red-painted toes and the toe ring. He looked back at the newspaper and finished off the sandwich.

Only Belle didn't move along to the bathroom, or to do whatever it was she'd come in the house to do. She stood there, her arms folded across her chest, skinny hip cocked.

He swallowed. Finished the glass of milk he was drinking.

She still hadn't moved.

He sighed. Folded the newspaper back along its creases. Crossed to the table to flip through the mail. Too many bills, circulars advertising some singles' matchmaking network, an expensive-looking envelope with an all too familiar embossed return address. He folded the envelope in half and shoved it in his back pocket. "What is it now?"

"I noticed that Lucy is still depending exclusively on her wheelchair."

The one remaining nerve not gone tight at the sight of the envelope now residing next to his butt joined the knotted rest. He opened a cupboard and grabbed the bottle of aspirin that had been full only a few weeks ago. He shook out a few, the rattle of pills inside the plastic sounding as sharp as his voice. "And?" He shut the cupboard door again only to find her extending a condensing bottle of water toward him.

"And it concerns me, because it's encouraging her to keep favoring her injury."

"She's not supposed to use her leg, yet." He swallowed the aspirin.

"She's not supposed to use it completely," Belle countered. "But she should have been up on crutches weeks ago, yet since I've been here—"

"Twenty-four hours now?"

"—I haven't even *seen* a pair of crutches. She does have them, doesn't she?"

Cage strode over to the tall, narrow closet at the end of the kitchen and snapped open the door. Inside, along with a broom and the vacuum cleaner, stood a shining new pair of crutches. "Satisfied?"

Her lips tightened. She flipped her long ponytail behind her shoulder and brushed past him to remove the crutches. He looked down at her, clutching the things to her chest. The top of her head didn't reach his chin. In fact, she wasn't much taller than Luce.

The realization didn't make Belle seem younger to him. It only made his daughter seem older.

He pushed the closet door shut and moved across the room. "She says that she still hurts too much to use 'em."

Belle nodded. "I understand, believe me. But getting on her feet with these is a major component of her recovery. And the longer we wait, the more it's going to hurt. You're going to have to get over trying to protect her, Cage. Her recuperation is *not* going to be pleasant all the time, but she does have to work through it before it'll get better." Her hand reached out and caught his forearm, squeezing in emphasis. "And it *will* get better." Then, seeming to realize that she was touching him, she quickly pulled back.

"Easy advice," he said flatly. "You ever watch *your* child trying to straighten or bend a leg that doesn't want to do either despite two separate surgeries that should have helped it? To steel yourself against the pleading in her eyes when she looks at you wanting permission to…just…stop?" If he'd expected her to look shocked at his unaccustomed outburst, he was wrong. Shock would've been better, though, than the expression softening her eyes. It was easier to take when she figured he avoided Lucy's sessions because of the never ending needs of the Lazy-B.

"I haven't watched *my* child," she said. "Since I've never even had one, that would be difficult." Then she suddenly lifted her foot onto one of the kitchen chairs and whipped the stretchy black pants that flared over her shoes up past her knee. The scar was old. Faded. It snaked down from beyond the folds of her pants on the inside of her taut thigh, circled her knee and disappeared down her calf. "But I have dealt with it myself."

The water and aspirin he'd just chugged mixed uncomfortably with his lunch. Lucy's healing surgical scars were bad. But when they healed, he knew they would look far better than Belle's.

"Not pretty," Belle murmured, and pulled her pant leg back down. "My hip doesn't look quite so bad."

"What happened?"

It was hard to believe it, but her brown eyes looked even darker. "I thought you knew."

"I suppose that's why you went into physical therapy," he surmised grudgingly.

"Yes." She sucked in one corner of her soft lip for a moment. Her expression was oddly still. "I was with my dad that night, Cage. The night of the accident."

He'd been wrong. His nerves *could* get tighter. "I didn't know you'd been hurt." He couldn't have known since her family had been living in Cheyenne at the time.

She studied the crutches she held. "I was lying down in the back seat. I didn't have on my seat belt, which my dad didn't know. When...it...happened, I was thrown from the car. Metal and flesh and bone. Don't mix well usually." She lifted her shoulder slightly. "Which is something you know only too well, I'm afraid. I'm sorry. I thought you knew," she said again then fell silent.

She looked miserable. And damned if he could convince himself it was an act, though he wanted to.

"Look, Cage, it's not too late for me to go. I know Lucy knows about the accident between our parents and she doesn't seem to hold it against my family. But everyone warned me this would be just one constant reminder after another." Her gaze whispered over him, then went back to the crutches. "I can hold my own against those opinions." Her voice was vaguely hoarse. "But if your feeling the same way gets in the path of Lucy's progress then my efforts here will be for nothing. Are...are you sure you want me to stay?"

No. He stared out the window. Lucy was sitting in

her chair just outside the barn, Strudel half in her lap while they played tug with a stick. "Lucy still needs help." His voice came from somewhere deep inside him.

He heard Belle sigh a little. "I could talk to the people I worked with at Huffington. Maybe I could find someone willing to—"

"No." He couldn't afford to bring someone else out to the ranch, to pay their full salary. Belle had been willing to agree for less than half what she deserved, and he knew it was only because of her fondness for his daughter. Something he'd deliberately capitalized on. The fact that she'd be able to provide the tutoring Lucy needed was even more of a bonus. "You came to help Lucy. I expect you to hold to your word."

"All right," she said after a long moment. She tucked her arm through the center of the crutches and carried them to the door. Then paused. "I'm really sorry your father didn't survive the accident, Cage."

"So am I," he said stiffly. He'd lost both his parents that night, even though his mother had technically survived. Apparently, the only one to escape unscathed that winter night nearly fourteen years ago had been the man who'd caused the accident in the first place.

Belle's father.

And even though he'd died a few years later, Belle was, after all, still his daughter.

Chapter Four

"I want to go with you."

Cage shook his head, ignoring Lucy's mutinous demand. "Not this time, Luce."

"Why not? I want to see Grandma."

He wished Belle wasn't standing at the kitchen sink washing up the pans she'd used to prepare Lucy's breakfast. He wished she'd stop doing things he wasn't paying her to do. She'd been under his roof for three days. He'd already warned her to stop dusting the shelves and mopping floors. They may have needed it, but when he'd come upon her doing the chores, he'd lit into her. More than necessary, he knew, but seeing her so at home in his house bugged him no end. He didn't want her being helpful. Not unless it was on his terms. "I'll take you to see her another time."

"When?"

"A few weeks."

Lucy's lips thinned. "I haven't seen her all summer."

"And nothing's changed." Her eyes widened a little at his sharp tone. He stifled a sigh. Before Lucy's fall, they'd gone every weekend. "Maybe this weekend. When Miss Day is off."

The prospect seemed enough to satisfy his daughter. "Miss Day's day off," Lucy quipped. Her lips tilted at the corners, thoroughly amused with herself and he felt his own lips twitch.

God, he loved the kid. "Yeah."

"Don't make fun of my name," Belle said lightly over the clink of dishes in the sink. "I grew up hearing every pun you could ever think of."

"Day isn't bad," Lucy countered. "You oughta hear what people used to call my dad."

Belle leaned her hip against the counter as she turned to look at them. The towel in her hand slowed over the plate she was drying. "Oh?"

"Yeah, Cage isn't his *real* name, you know. Who would name their kid *that?*"

Cage caught his daughter's gaze, lifting his eyebrow in only a partially mock warning. "Did you make your bed?"

Lucy laughed. But she took the hint and didn't pursue the topic of Cage's first name. She lifted her arms and he automatically started to reach for her to transfer her from the chair at the table to her wheelchair. But he caught Belle's look.

How to protect someone in the long run by causing them pain now? He felt the humor sparked by his daughter drain away and instead of lifting her, he handed her the crutches that were leaning against the wall.

"Dad." Lucy pouted.

"Lucy," Belle prompted gently. "We've talked about this."

He supposed that wasn't surprising. If she'd taken him to task about the crutches, she'd probably done the same with his daughter. Understanding the reasons was one thing. Liking it another.

Lucy took the crutches. Belle set down the towel and helped the girl to her feet. With the crutches tucked beneath her arms, Lucy looked at Cage. "She told me not to pout around you 'cause you were too much of a marshmallow to hold out against me." Then she shot Belle a look before awkwardly swinging out of the kitchen.

Belle's cheeks were pink and she quickly turned back to the dishes.

Cage filled a coffee mug with the fragrant stuff she'd made earlier, damning the consequences, and watched her for a moment. She was wearing another pair of those thin, long pants. Jazz pants, he knew, because he'd had to buy some for Lucy for something her dance class had done last winter.

Today, Belle's pants were as red as a tomato. She wore a sleeveless top in the same color that hugged her torso and zipped all the way up to her throat.

She'd have been about Lucy's age when the accident happened. How long had it taken her to recover from *her* injuries?

He abruptly finished off his coffee. Learning that she'd been hurt in the same accident as his parents didn't change anything. Gus Day had killed his father on a stretch of highway outside of Cheyenne, pure and simple. He sat the emptied mug down with a thunk. "Marsh-mallow?"

"She wasn't supposed to tell you that."

"She's still young. She hasn't learned the art of discretion."

"She's learned a lot of other things. If you're worried that going with you to Cheyenne today will be too taxing, don't. She's up to the trip."

He'd told Belle and Lucy that he was making the drive when they'd both stopped in surprise at finding him in the kitchen that morning instead of already out for the day as he usually was. "It's business," he said again. True enough in a sense. Personal business. The kind he wasn't inclined to share, not even with Lucy. Not until he was forced to. "I probably won't be back until late."

Belle didn't look happy.

"I told you that I can have Emmy Johannson come over to watch her."

"And I told you that would be ridiculous since I'm staying here anyway. You want to have the argument you've been spoiling for now that Lucy's out of range?" She shot him a look, her eyebrows arched, and when he said nothing, she deliberately dried another plate. Short of yanking it out of her hands there wasn't much he could do about it. "I'm not going to twiddle my thumbs between sessions and lessons, Cage, but that wasn't what I was trying to get at anyway. Has it occurred to you that maybe Lucy wants to be where *you* are?"

"She wants to see my mother. And this discussion is over." Maybe he couldn't keep her from washing the damn dishes, but he didn't have to listen to advice unrelated to Lucy's rehabilitation.

Belle shrugged and focused on the dishes again, seeming not to turn one hair of her thick brown pony-tail at his decree. But her lashes guarded her eyes. And he damned all over again the turn of events that had prompted him to bring her into this house.

A timely reminder of why he was going to Cheyenne in the first place.

He rose and grabbed his hat off the hook. "Luce has my cell-phone number," he said as he strode from the room. He thought he heard her murmur "drive carefully" after him, but couldn't be sure.

Lucy was in her bathroom when he hunted her down to tell her he was leaving. He rapped on the door. "Behave yourself," he said through the wood.

She yanked open the door, leaning heavily on her crutches. "What else is there to do," she asked tartly. "You won't let me go near the horses anymore."

"When I'm sure you're not going to go near *that* horse, I'll consider it."

"You're *never* going to let me ride Satin again, are you?"

It was an old refrain and one he didn't want to be pulled into singing. "Make sure you feed Strudel," he said. "And do the exercises on your own that Miss Day says you're supposed to be doing.

"I hate doing them. They hurt. And they're boring." Her face was mutinous. An expression that had been too frequent of late.

"I'm sorry they hurt, but I don't care if they're boring," he said mildly. "They're necessary."

Her jaw worked. Her eyes rolled. Then all the fight drained out of her and she gave him a beseeching look. "How come you won't let me go with you today?"

Dammit, he *was* a marshmallow where she was concerned. But not this time. "You got a problem hanging around here with Miss Day?"

Lucy rolled her eyes again. "Jeez, Dad. Her name is Belle. And *no* I don't have a problem with her. Not like *you* do, anyway."

"I don't have a problem with Miss Day."

"Right. That's why you watch her like you do. You oughta just ask her out on a date or something."

"I do not want to date Miss Day," he assured evenly and gently tugged the end of her braid as he leaned down to kiss her forehead. "Behave."

She grimaced. "Like there's anything else you'd let me do? Say 'hi' to Grandma for me."

He nodded as he headed out. If he did go by the care center, he'd pass on the greeting, but he knew there would be no reciprocation, which was the very reason why he would *never* want to date Miss Day.

"Have you ever been in love, Belle?"

The question came out of the blue and Belle looked up from Lucy's leg. "Is the cramp gone?"

Lucy nodded, gingerly flexing her toes.

It was evening and they were back in the barn again. Cage hadn't yet returned from Cheyenne.

"So, have you?"

Belle leaned back and grabbed a hand towel, wiping the remains of oil she'd been using from her palms. "Yes."

"With who?"

Belle flicked Lucy with the end of the towel and rolled to her feet. The CD had ended and she exchanged it for another. "Howie Bloom," she said.

"Howie?" Lucy echoed.

"We were in second grade together. I thought he was the perfect man. He, however, thought Nikki was the perfect woman."

"They liked each other?"

"Nikki told him to take a hike. She'd never have poached on what I considered my territory."

"I wish I had a sister," Lucy grumbled dramatically. She flopped back on the blue mats, flinging her arms wide, before slowly moving them up and down. If she'd been in the snow, she would have been making snow angels. Belle wondered if the girl even knew she was partially moving her legs—both of them—as well, and decided not to point it out. It wasn't the first time she'd noticed Lucy unconsciously using her injured leg.

"Instead, I'm all alone," Lucy lamented. "With dad. I think he needs a woman. Then mebbe he wouldn't be on my case all the time."

Belle sank her teeth into her tongue for a moment and when the urge to snort passed, she chanced speaking. "If your dad wants to be with someone, I'm sure nothing would stop him." It seemed a safe enough response. And Lord knew the man was attractive. For a grouch.

"I s'pose. He could'a dated Anya's mom. They were in school together when they were little. But she got engaged to Mr. Pope. Dad's way hotter than he is."

Larry Pope was a teacher at the high school. A perfectly nice man, what little Belle knew of him. She seriously doubted anyone in Weaver muttered *ogre* behind his back. But he wasn't in the same hemisphere of hot that Cage Buchanan occupied.

Which was neither here nor there, Belle reminded herself.

"Then Anya and I would be sisters. But Dad never looked at Mrs. Johannson like…you know."

"And Anya is away visiting her dad?"

Lucy nodded. "'Til next month." She exhaled, sounding utterly dejected.

Belle pushed to her feet and held out her hands. "Come on. Let's go make popcorn and watch movies." Lucy had a sizable collection of videotapes in her bedroom from which to choose. Maybe one of them would provide enough distraction that she'd stop wondering what kind of woman Cage did look at like *you know*.

Cage could see the blue-tinted glow through the living-room windows as he finally drove up to the house that night. Television was on. It was after midnight.

He parked near the back of the house. Sat there in the dark, listening to the tick of his cooling engine. Unlike the bluish light coming from the window at the front of the house, the light he could see from the upstairs one looked golden. Either Belle had fallen asleep with the light on, or she was still awake. Probably the reason for that blue glow downstairs.

He blew out a long breath and grabbed the manila envelope that had been his companion on the long drive up from Cheyenne and headed inside. His trip had been successful only in giving him some breathing room.

Hopefully.

The aroma of buttery popcorn met him. Two bowls—one empty, one nearly so—sat on the table.

He hadn't stopped for dinner before driving back and grabbed a handful from the remains. Lightly doused with Parmesan cheese. Lucy's doing, he figured. Kid liked the stuff on everything.

The low murmur of voices and familiar music from the television kept the house from being entirely silent. He went into the living room. Lucy, tangled up with her favorite pink blanket, was sprawled over most of the couch. And Belle, as well, since her legs were tossed over Belle's lap.

His daughter didn't budge as he walked in the room. She was asleep.

"Did your trip go well?" Belle's voice was soft.

He finally let himself look at her. Only long enough to see that she was wrapped in a bulky white robe that was falling open at the base of her long neck. "It went. City seems to get busier every time I drive down there. You probably can't wait to get back there, I suppose."

"That's the plan," she agreed evenly.

He eyed her for a moment. She hadn't said anything, but she had to think his place was stuck somewhere two decades past.

God. What a mood he was in. "How long's Luce been asleep?"

"Since Ariel got her legs."

He glanced at the television. Judging by the stack of videos on top of it, he knew this movie hadn't been the first they'd watched. *The Little Mermaid* might not be recent, but it'd been Lucy's favorite Disney flick since the day she first saw it. "She hasn't made it through that video without falling asleep since she was five."

"Didn't hurt that she worked pretty hard today."

"You told me you'd be doing all the same exercises she does, right alongside her."

"Yes. But I'm not working at a disadvantage the way she currently is."

Memories of Lucy growing up battled for space in his mind against memories from his own youth. He'd believed none of the Days had been affected by the accident. God knew, Gus Day had never said a word of it during the few times he'd tried contacting Cage afterward. Now, he knew Belle had been hurt, as well. He dropped his envelope on the ancient coffee table and leaned over the couch.

Belle sucked in her breath, unable to prevent the reaction when he moved so suddenly. But he gave no notice. Simply slid his arms under his daughter, hands impersonally skimming Belle's thighs in the process, before lifting Lucy's limp form easily against his chest. She swallowed and tried not to be obvious about clutching the comforting folds of her robe together over her legs. She needn't have worried what Cage would think, however, since he was already carrying his daughter down the hall toward her bedroom, the pink blanket trailing around his long legs.

She'd seen his expression one too many times when he looked at his daughter. Naked devotion.

On the television, Sebastian was beseeching the prince to kiss the girl, and Belle hit the remote, stopping the singing crab midnote. She was tidying up the scattered napkins and loose kernels of popped corn from the coffee table when Cage returned. "Did she wake up?"

He shook his head and closed his long fingers over his envelope before she could move it out of her way. "Except for the nightmares, it takes something cataclysmic to wake her up in the middle of the night."

She wasn't sure if it was censure she heard in his voice, or not. But they hadn't discussed Lucy's bedtime, so she could honestly say she hadn't deliberately flaunted his rules. She also could honestly say that standing there with him in the hushed light of the snowy television screen seemed suddenly, abruptly, far too personal. As he was fond of pointing out, she was there to do a job. Wondering what in the package—with its embossed return address for an attorney in Cheyenne— was responsible for the tense muscle flexing in his jaw wasn't part of that job.

"Well. It *is* the middle of the night." She lifted her cupped hands a little. "I'll just throw this stuff away." But he was pretty much blocking the way to the kitchen because there was little room to maneuver between the couch and table. She pressed her lips together for a moment, awkwardly waiting for him to shift aside. When he finally did, she hurried past him and dropped her handful of trash in the garbage can beneath the kitchen sink. She rinsed and dried her hands, then remembered the bowls on the table and started for them. But Cage beat her to it, handing her only the empty one even as he shoved his other hand in the leftovers.

"Luce didn't put so much parmesan on her popcorn this time," he murmured before popping some into his mouth. "It's still edible for once."

Belle pushed her lips into a smile. Maybe he was oblivious to the fact that she was wearing her robe, but she was not. And the popcorn he was devouring hadn't been Lucy's, it had been hers. "Yes. Well. Good night." Gloria Day had drilled manners into her daughters, prompting the polite words when her most immediate desire was to simply run up to the safety of her bedroom. He, however, didn't return the sentiment and she thought he wouldn't as she headed into the hall.

"Belle."

Why did he only know her name when his home was bathed in midnight shadows? She caught her hand around the door jamb. "Yes?"

"Thanks for watching Luce today."

It really was the very last thing she might have expected from him. Surprise softened her for a moment until she gathered herself. "You're welcome."

He nodded once, and that seemed to be the end of it. Of course, he was plowing through the remains of her popcorn as if he were starving. "Did you eat dinner?"

He'd leaned one hip against the counter, cradling the popcorn bowl against his stomach. "This is fine." Which was no answer at all.

"There are leftovers in the fridge."

Information that didn't seem to fill him with glee.

"I made some hamburger-casserole thing," she added. "Didn't have a name, but Lucy said it was one of her favorites. The recipe was in the recipe box in your cupboard." It had taken her a while to gather her nerves to even open the little metal box that was crammed with yellowed newsprint recipes as well as neatly hand-printed recipe cards. It was in keeping with the other aging, but homey, touches the house still possessed.

"That was my mother's recipe box."

Exactly what Belle had assumed, and why she'd hesitated. "I hope you don't mind. Anyway, that's what I fixed. It has hamburger and carrots and potatoes and—"

"Yeah." He set aside the bowl and watched her, his hooded expression too shadowed to read. "My mother used to fix it for us. It was my father's favorite, too."

And wasn't that a handy way to put a stop to their awkward conversation? "There's plenty left for you," she said and continued down the hallway to the staircase.

Upstairs in the bedroom, she felt an urge to call her sister, but didn't. Just because she was having a hard time sleeping under Cage Buchanan's roof didn't mean she needed to share the problem by interrupting Nikki's sleep, as well.

She tossed her robe over the wooden chair in the corner and climbed into bed before snapping off the lamp sitting on the nightstand. Every time she closed her eyes, though, she saw Cage in her mind's eye. Striding toward the house, lean hipped and long legged in worn jeans, his cowboy hat set on his bronzy head at a no-nonsense angle. Wolfing popcorn. Carrying his daughter.

She scooched down the bed. Scrunched up her pillow this way and that. Turned from one side onto her other.

Then sat bolt upright when she heard the brisk knock on her door. "Yes?" Oh, stupid, Belle. She should have gotten up and put on the robe. Instead, she sat there in bed, tangled in sheet and quilt while the bedroom door opened and Cage appeared.

She couldn't summon so much as a coherent thought or word as he entered the room, walking right across to her.

Then he suddenly knelt, one hand braced on the mattress only inches from her bare knee. The mattress dipped and the springs gave out a loud moan.

For some reason, she felt as if they'd been caught doing something…intimate.

"What—" Finally her tongue loosened. "What are you doing?" But his head just kept going lower.

She leaned over, grabbing the sheet up against her chest, flinging it more fully over her leg to see him actually slipping beneath the high-set bed. "Looking for the boogeyman?"

He had a small can in his hand, she realized. "You creak." His voice was muffled.

"Only in the mornings when I first get out of bed," she muttered.

She heard a soft spraying sound, followed by a hint of an oily scent. Then he was pushing out from beneath the bed again, and levering himself to his feet. "The bedsprings."

"I noticed."

He headed to the door. "So did I."

A statement that was disturbing only because it made her wonder what he was doing on his side of the wall that he could hear *her* bedsprings creaking. Did he listen for her as closely as she listened for him, hoping to avoid running into him? Bad enough to know she hid out in this very room early every morning until the sounds of him moving around in his room, then showering in the bathroom, were long gone.

He stopped at the door and glanced back. The light from the hallway spilled around his broad shoulders. "And, so you know, you don't have to keep hiding the scars on your leg."

She blinked.

"If Luce sees that you're self-conscious about yours, she's going to be the same way about hers," he continued abruptly. Then he closed the door.

Belle flopped back on the bed. The bedsprings gave one halfhearted creak, then were silent.

Of course. His only concern was Lucy.

Chapter Five

"Did you ask your dad yet about having a birthday party?"

Lucy shook her head, apparently too intent on painting her toenails—pink, of course—to answer. They were taking a break from studying and Lucy was sitting on the floor in her bedroom, leaning over with the polish brush.

"Why not?" Belle tucked the tip of her tongue between her teeth watching the way Lucy compensated for her injured knee. Lucy was unusually limber, which in general was a plus, but occasionally—when she would ordinarily be forced to make her leg try harder—she could work around it. Which was something she nearly always did. Even though she'd made faces and grumbled about their actual therapy sessions in the five days since they'd begun, she hadn't been completely obstreperous, which Belle had initially feared. What interested Belle even more, though, was the fact that when she was just going through her ordinary day Lucy accomplished ever so much more. Unconsciously.

Lucy still hadn't answered her question, though. "Hey there." She leaned over, looking into Lucy's absorbed face. "Why haven't you asked him, yet? You said yesterday that you were going to." And the day before that, and the day before that.

"He won't let me have any boys come and if no boys come, then none of the girls will want to come, either."

"Do *you* want boys to come?" Belle idly plucked a bottle of clear polish out of Lucy's collection and shook it a few times before unscrewing the top.

"Anya's gonna want Ryan to come."

Belle flattened her hand on the top of a teen magazine and began stroking the clear polish over her fingernails. Ryan, she knew, was Ryan Clay. Her nephew by virtue of her mother's marriage into the Clay family. "Okay, so I know what Anya wants, but what about you?"

Lucy straightened, and lifted one shoulder as she put the cap back on her polish and tossed it back in the pretty, lacquered box that contained her modest assortment of polishes. "I dunno."

Belle switched hands to paint the rest of her nails. "My old boss used to call me *bulldog*," she murmured. "Because I don't give up very easily. So why don't you just tell me what's really holding you back on having a party? Otherwise, I'll just have to keep asking."

"Bulldog?" Lucy looked skeptical. "You're making that up."

"I can call Nikki and she'll tell you I'm not. She's Mr. Reed's assistant, and he tends to give everyone a nickname."

"How come you don't still work there?"

"Oh, I'll be going back," Belle assured her with a blitheness she was far from feeling. "I'm sort of on vacation."

"So, you won't be at my school next year?"

Belle shook her head.

"Then how can you tell me we'll work on something other than dancing for the talent contest?"

"We've got the rest of summer vacation to figure it out for you."

"But then you'll be leaving."

Belle heard loneliness underlying Lucy's matter-of-fact tone. And why wouldn't she be lonely? Living on a remote ranch. No company other than a dog, a television and videos, a horse she wasn't supposed to go around and a father who worked from sunup to sundown. Other than the day he'd gone to Cheyenne, Cage had been noticeably absent around the house.

He'd even stopped complaining that Belle was cooking meals for his daughter, and had stopped coming in, himself, to make sure Lucy had lunch. "Yes," she finally answered honestly. "I'll be leaving. Because you're going to be running circles around me by then and you won't need me anymore. But we'll still be friends, sweetie. You can call me anytime."

"Do you and Nikki live together in Cheyenne?"

"Lord, no. I love my sister, but we'd drive each other mad in two days flat. We're only a few blocks away from each other, though. She has this beautiful town house that she's been decorating herself. I have an apartment that is completely standard issue. Well, I *had* an apartment." She hadn't renewed her lease when it expired, because she'd been in Weaver, by then. Instead, with the help of Nikki and some friends, she'd moved her few personal items of furniture into the little house in Weaver where she was staying. "I'll have to find a new place to live when I go back there." She smiled, determined to cheer the solemn look from Lucy's face. "Maybe your dad will let you come and visit me there, even."

"Really?"

"Of course."

But Lucy's sharply hopeful moment was brief. "Dad won't let me, anyway."

Belle stopped fanning her hands and tested the polish. Dry. "Enough of that. Your dad seems pretty willing to do back flips for you."

"He won't let me go see my grandparents."

"He said he would think about taking you to Cheyenne to visit your grandmother this weekend."

"My other grandparents. The Oldham side." Lucy dropped the lid back on the lacquered box and lifted it onto her legs. Her hand smoothed over the fine surface. "My grandmother sent this to me a few months ago. Dad nearly had a cow."

"Maybe he's not comfortable with his little girl being old enough to wear nail polish. Dads can be that way sometimes." Hers certainly had been.

"That's what *he* said."

"Well. There you go." Belle's mind was busy, turning over the notion of Lucy's maternal grandparents.

The only thing the rumor mill had produced on them was that they were wealthy. "Have they invited you to visit or something?"

Lucy shook her head. "Not really. I just—we've talked a couple times on the phone. Dad doesn't know, though."

Belle wished Lucy hadn't imparted that little tidbit, but the girl was continuing. "They live in Chicago. They're the ones who sent me Satin, too."

The horse that had thrown Lucy.

"Isn't Chicago where that performing-arts school you were interested in is located?"

"Yeah." Lucy leaned her head back against the foot of her bed. "Guess it didn't matter that Dad wouldn't let me go on that field trip there. Even if I could have gotten to visit the school during one of the free days, they wouldn't want me like this."

"Satin hadn't thrown you yet when the field trip was scheduled. Even so, it doesn't mean the school wouldn't want you when you *are* ready again," Belle pointed out.

Lucy just shrugged again. Then she set aside the lacquered box and turned, pulling herself up onto the bed. She grabbed the crutches propped beside her and braced her weight against them to push to her feet. "Even if I earned a scholarship, he wouldn't let me go." She slowly clumped out of the bedroom.

This is what she got for becoming personally involved with a patient, Belle thought, watching the girl leave. Instead of just being concerned with rehabilitating a body, she began wanting to fix everything else, too. And while she didn't know whether or not Lucy would be better served by going to a private school so far away from home, she *did* know that Lucy was uncommonly talented.

She slid back into her shoes, grabbed Lucy's discarded tennies, too, and went after her. "Come on," she said when she found Lucy leaning against the kitchen counter, staring out the window. "We've explored all over the Lazy-B this past week except for one place." She waved Lucy's shoes. "Sit and put these on."

"There's only one place we haven't gone."

"Right. The stables."

"Dad doesn't think I should go down there."

Belle nodded. "Unsupervised," she improvised, remembering Cage's words. But Lucy's mood had been in the dumps long enough and Belle was tired of trying to catch Cage to talk to him about her observations where his daughter was concerned. Including her suspicion that Lucy's reluctant attitude toward her recovery was somehow related to the horse that had thrown her. "His point is that he doesn't want you trying to ride yet, and I agree with him. Your muscles are nowhere near ready for the strain of a horse's girth. But visiting is not riding. And you've got more horses than just Satin, right?"

Lucy looked vaguely skeptical, which didn't do a lot for Belle's tinge of uncertainty. But it was the middle of the afternoon. If Cage's habit held, he wouldn't make an appearance until it was nearly dark. It wasn't that Belle intended to get away with something. She'd let Cage know, after the fact, that they'd visited the horses, and that doing so had lifted Lucy's spirits. If he had a quarrel with *that,* she'd deal with it.

She was suddenly impatient to get going before she lost her nerve, and crouched down to tie Lucy's shoes, herself. And when that was done, she brought out the wheelchair that was mostly stored in the corner of the kitchen these days. "You can ride this time." The stables were considerably farther out from the house than the barn was. "Bring the crutches, though."

Lucy looked relieved to shift into the chair. She propped the long crutches against the metal footrest and her shoulder, and they went out through the front, to use the ramp.

The summer afternoon was hot, and Belle was perspiring by the time she'd pushed Lucy all the way to the stables. "Too bad you don't have a swimming hole around here," she said as they entered the shade of the stable. "We could use a little cooling off." She doubted that Cage would grant Belle permission to take his daughter out to the ranch her mother lived on with Squire. The Double-C had a great swimming hole.

Maybe she'd look into driving Lucy into Braden. The town was some distance from Weaver, but there was a public pool there. And swimming would be good for Lucy's leg.

"That's Rory," Lucy pointed out as they passed an SUV parked in the space of what would be two stalls and came to the first horse. "He's older 'n I am."

The big buckskin stuck his head over the rail, nudging at Lucy's outstretched hand. "I should have brought carrots." She braced the rubber tips of her crutches against the hard-packed earth that formed the aisle between the stalls and stood. Belle stepped around the chair and slowly walked down one side of the aisle with Lucy. At each stall, they stopped. Lucy greeted the horses as if they were long-lost friends.

It was practically heartbreaking.

Then they got to the last stall in the row.

Satin, Belle immediately knew. Aptly named because she'd never seen a more beautiful black. It was as if Black Beauty had stepped right out of the pages of the classic novel. "Oh…my," she murmured. She'd been around horses her entire life as a pleasure rider, but she'd never seen such a magnificent animal.

Lucy was hanging back slightly but as soon as she realized that Belle noticed, she tossed her head and continued forward as if her hesitation had never happened at all. "Satin Finish," Lucy said. "He's seventeen hands. Sired out of Knotty Wood. He was a Triple-Crown winner."

Belle started. "A *racehorse?*"

"Satin's never raced, though." Lucy started to reach for the horse, but stayed the movement, never quite touching him.

What on earth was a horse bred like that doing on a working cattle ranch? Belle found it unfathomable. "He's quite a gift. Is he being ridden at all?"

"No, and he's not going to be."

The deep voice was flat. But the fury in it was unmistakable, and Belle nearly jumped right out of her skin. She was faintly aware of Lucy reacting similarly as they both whirled around, feeling caught and guilty as sin, in the face of Cage's towering disapproval.

It wasn't directed at his daughter, though. His fiercely blue gaze rested on Lucy for only a moment, obviously seeing that she was perfectly fine, before settling on Belle. "What…the…hell…do you think you are doing?"

She very nearly quailed. She'd known she was taking a chance on angering him. But Lucy's recovery mattered more. She clasped her hands together behind her back. She could feel Satin's huffing breath at the nape of her neck. "I asked Lucy to introduce me to her friends here in the stable."

"Lucy, go wait for me in the truck."

"But—"

"*Go.*"

The girl sidled along the row until she passed her father, then she quickly swung herself down the aisle to the dusty brown pickup truck Belle could see parked at the end.

Belle started, watching the girl's movements. The moment they heard the click of the truck door closing, Cage stepped toward Belle and she nervously took a step back, only to feel the iron rails of the stall press against her shoulder. Satin began nibbling at her ponytail.

She shifted, quickly pulling her hair out of the reach of temptation. She was undoubtedly safer with the horse's attention, though, than with Cage's.

"The first day you came here," he said, his voice deadly quiet. "What about our conversation that day did you not understand?"

"I'm not a horse thief." The stab at lessening the tension failed miserably.

"You'd be better off at the moment if you were. You could steal *that*—" he jerked his chin toward Satin "—and I'd applaud you all the way to the state line."

Belle stiffened her spine. "So what are you going to do? Glare and stride around all heavy booted and

macho? For heaven's sake, Cage, did you even notice
what Lucy did a few minutes ago?"

"I *noticed* she was ten inches away from that spawn
of a horse," he snapped. "He's unpredictable. I don't
need to worry about something else taking my daughter away from me, too."

"She put weight on her foot!" Her hands clenched.
Unclenched. "What do you mean, *too?*"

He glared at her, his jaw flexing. "Satan—"

"—Satin."

"—*Satan,*" he repeated, "threw her once. She's a
good rider, and she could have been killed."

"But she wasn't," Belle reminded him slowly. "And
if you hate the horse so much—think he's such a danger even when he's not being ridden—why is he still
here?"

He turned away from her as if he couldn't stand the
sight of her. "Lucy would hate me more than I hate that
horse if I got rid of him."

His admission was so raw it tore at her. She pressed
her lips together for a moment, scrambling for the objectivity that she was supposed to have. "Lucy says that
she wants to get better. But something is holding her
back during her sessions, Cage."

"And your answer to that is tempting her back onto
that horse."

That horse nickered softly and tossed his head,
brushing hard enough against Belle's shoulder to make
her stumble forward. She caught herself before she
knocked right into Cage. "I wasn't doing anything of
the sort," Belle defended. "And Lucy doesn't want to
get *on* Satin, anyway."

"She bugs me about it constantly."

"Then it's an act!"

"You can't tell that."

"I can," she assured evenly, "as easily as I can see that she's deliberately holding herself back in our sessions. And if you weren't so intent on avoiding me, I'd have talked to you about all this already!"

His expression was plain. He didn't believe her.

Frustration churned inside her. "You'd see it, Cage, if you took more than five minutes out of your day to spend with her. I know why you avoid me, but to avoid Lucy, too, is ridiculous. When you and I first met, I thought you were just a stubborn dad who wasn't ready to let his child go off on a field trip so far away from home."

"That field trip to Chicago was planned a year in advance, and Lucy knew all along I wasn't going to let her go." He leaned over her. "You were interfering then and you're interfering now."

"Well, maybe you *need* some interfering around here! You know, half the population of Weaver considers you an ogre, but I didn't want to believe it. Goodness knows, the people around here have known you a lot longer than I have. So maybe they're more accurate than I am! As far as I'm concerned, keeping the stable off limits to Lucy because you're jealous of a horse given to her by her grandparents isn't overprotective or stubborn. It's cruel."

She brushed past him, knowing the words shouldn't have left her lips, but there was no way to retract them. Instead, they lingered there, silently following as she strode out of the shadows into the lengthening afternoon light.

He'd fire her now, for sure. And maybe that was just fine with her.

But she stopped, seeing Lucy sitting in the truck, her young features pinched into worried lines.

Belle veered back toward the vehicle, propping her hands on the opened window. "Don't worry," she said huskily. "It's me your dad is angry with, not you."

"He better not fire you," Lucy said, throwing her arms around Belle's neck. "I'll hate him forever if he does!"

Belle smoothed her hand down Lucy's gilded head. "You're not going to hate him." She'd once told her father she'd hated him, with devastating results. "And he hasn't fired me." Yet. She didn't even dare look over her shoulder to see if he was bearing down on her to deliver that very coup de grâce. But, of course, she had to.

She looked back.

Cage was still standing by Satin's stall, his hands braced against the top rail, his head lowered. Strudel danced around his legs for a moment, but he didn't even seem to notice, and eventually the dog skittered away from Satin's vicinity to jump at a woven blanket hanging off a high hook.

Belle pressed her cheek against Lucy's blond head and closed her eyes, but Cage's image was seared into her mind, as clear as a painting.

Man at end of rope it was titled. And it made her heart simply ache.

"It'll be okay," she murmured to Lucy. If she had more guts, she'd approach Cage. Apologize. Try to make amends. Again. Either he'd fire her or he wouldn't, and that would be the end of it.

He still hadn't moved.

And she wasn't brave enough, after all, to take a dose of his bitterness, no matter how deserved. "I'm going to drive back into town," she told Lucy. It was a few hours earlier than she would have left for her weekend off, but just then, the idea seemed prudent.

Lucy caught her hands. "Are you going to come back?"

She forced a smile. "Monday through Friday. That's the deal."

She looked back again at Cage. Belle simply had to believe that things *would* work out.

For all of them.

Chapter Six

She was out in her yard, hunched over a lawn mower.

Cage parked across the street next to the sidewalk bordering Weaver Park and the school and cut the engine. He unhooked his sunglasses from the rearview mirror and slid them on. But his gaze didn't waver from Belle Day puttering about in her small front yard.

Annoying. Interfering. Too sexy for such a scrawny thing. He'd expected those things when he'd hired her, because he'd thought those things from the first day they'd met when she'd cornered him about that damn field trip.

So, he'd expected all that. Been prepared for all that. Been ready to have the daughter of a man he'd hated for longer than his adult life living under his roof because he was beyond desperate to prove to a passel of lawyers that nobody—not even two people rich enough to buy heaven—could provide a better home for his daughter than he could.

He *hadn't* been ready for his daughter to become the woman's champion. Hadn't been ready for Lucy's tearful accusations—when he'd discovered her actually doing her small exercises on her own without him having to get on her case about it—that he'd scared off Belle Day for good. Damn sure hadn't expected to come after the woman, two days later hat in hand.

She was sitting on the grass now, banging at the mower. The metallic noise rang out, sounding out of place in the morning air.

He got out of his truck and crossed the empty street. Down a few doors, a trio of kids played in a picket-fenced yard. The other direction, a teenage boy was slopping a sudsy rag over a shining red car.

He couldn't ever remember feeling as young as they looked. Or as young as Belle looked, for that matter, though he knew she was only a few years younger than he was.

Maybe that's what a man got for inheriting an adult's responsibilities when he was sixteen.

He rolled the sleeves of his shirt farther up his arms as he stepped up on the sidewalk. He could hear Belle muttering colorful curses under her breath. It was almost amusing. "What's the problem?"

She jerked, craning her head around. A tangle of emotions crossed her face. "Won't start." She turned back to the mower. The ends of her ponytail flirted with the faint breeze, dancing around the waist of her faded jeans.

Cage walked around to the other side. Splotches of black grease covered her hands. A few more clangs rang out courtesy of her banging. "That helping?" His voice was dry.

She angled him a look as she tugged up the halter strap of her red bikini top. "Does it look like it? What are you doing here?" Her chin set and she looked back down at the engine. She had a smudge of grease on her collarbone, now. "As if I can't guess."

He bent his knees, hunkering down next to the mower. Better to look at the engine. He slid the wrench out of her unresisting fingers. Just because he was there didn't mean the words weren't sitting in his throat fit to choke him. "I brought Luce into town. She's at Emmy Johansson's."

"Stored there all safe and sound where I can't lead her down danger's path?" She grabbed the wrench back from him. "You're all dressed up. You're going to get greasy."

A clean gray shirt and black jeans was dressed up? She must really think he was a hick. "Luce told me you weren't going to let her ride."

"I told you that, too." She unwound her crossed legs and knelt, leaning over the mower as she strained to remove the housing.

God. He had a straight view down her lithe torso and she had no clue whatsoever. Her nipples were as hard as—

He looked across the street to the park.

She huffed and sat back down on her butt, stretching out her legs. "This is hopeless."

Hopeless was getting the branded image of her breasts out of his head. "She also implied you wouldn't be back on Monday. Give me the wrench."

She eyed him. "Is that the newest euphemism for telling someone to go...soak your head?"

"I heard that Colby's has an open-mike night on Saturdays," he said blandly. "You can try out the stand-up comedy there."

She flipped up the wrench like a one-fingered salute. "And take away your spotlight?"

"Funny." He didn't go to Colby's and they both knew it. Next to Ruby's Diner, Colby's was the best stop for buffalo wings, beer and gossip. He preferred beef, didn't drink beer or anything else alcoholic and couldn't abide wagging tongues. He grabbed the wrench. Studied the mower for a moment then easily unfastened the housing and set it aside.

"Show-off," Belle muttered.

"You're welcome."

She snatched the wrench back once more. "If you've come to fire me, just get it done and over with. As you can see—" she waved her hand beyond the mower to her slightly overgrown grass "—I have things to do." She tugged at the halter strap again and leaned over the mower. She stuck her fingers here and there, poking and plucking and he knew she didn't have a single clue what she was doing.

Irritation rippled along his spine. "I didn't come to fire you. I told you what Lucy said. I came to make sure you didn't quit on me. Don't stick your finger in there." He pushed her hands out of the way, but she didn't move so easily. And now, his hands were as greasy as hers.

She swatted at him. "It's *my* mower!"

He closed his fingers around hers. "So I should just sit here and let you ruin the chances of ever fixing it?"

Her eyebrows peaked. Their fingers felt glued together by the sticky grease.

Heat collected at the base of his spine, shooting right up it, threatening his sanity. He let her go.

She sat back, her wrists propped on her knees, gooey fingers splayed. "Well." Her voice was a little husky. "There's a concept."

"My daughter is not a bloody lawn mower. And you need a new spark plug."

"I *know* your daughter isn't yard equipment." She shook her head, looking disgusted. "So, you came because you're afraid I'm a quitter."

"Are you?"

"I don't quit on people I care about," she said after a moment.

"Admirable. What about Lucy?"

She huffed. "I care about *her.*"

"And not me."

Her eyebrows rose again over brown eyes that looked too vulnerable for comfort. "Wouldn't that be the height of folly? It really must have frosted your cookies when Days began moving to your neck of the woods, instead of staying nice and faraway in Cheyenne. Do you loathe the Clays, too, since Squire had the bad form to marry my mother?"

"Does that mean you're in Weaver permanently?" She started to reach for the housing, but he beat her to it, mostly out of pity for the equipment. In seconds, the mower was assembled.

"No," she said fervently. "Believe me, I cannot *wait* to go back to my job at the clinic in Cheyenne. If you didn't live out on the Lazy-B like some hermit, you'd probably know that. As a topic for gossip, I'm as much fair game as anyone else who lives here." She stood and started to grab the mower, but stopped, looking beyond him with a grimace. "Oh, great."

"Problems, Belle?" A cheerful female voice assaulted them.

Cage looked over and saw Brenda Wyatt practically skipping down the sidewalk, she was in such a hurry to get the latest scoop. "Speaking of gossip," he muttered under his breath.

"Nothing major," Belle assured the woman, ignoring him.

"Anything I can help with?" Brenda stopped shy of stepping on the grass, her eyes curious and sharp as a hungry bird.

"Not unless your husband has a spare spark plug for this thing." Belle nudged the mower with her tennis shoe.

"Well, I'll just go and see." Brenda's gaze rested on Cage for a moment. He could practically see the speculation turning inside her head. Then she smiled again, and hurried back toward her picketed yard.

"Now she's gonna feel compelled to come back, you know."

Belle's smile was mocking. "So? Nobody's asking you to stay. Consider your brief presence here your good deed for the day. It'll provide hours and hours of entertainment for Brenda."

"Is this what it's gonna be like now if you come back to the Lazy-B?" He still had some doubts that she'd return, because she hadn't actually said she would. "Open warfare?"

"You're the one who declared it, Cage."

"Thought you wanted to maintain some civility for Lucy's sake."

"All I was trying to do was help. That's all I've ever wanted to do. But you've either treated me like a leper or a liar. I'm sorry for the past, Cage. More than you can possibly know. Maybe you think you're being disloyal to your father's memory, or to your mother, by employing the enemy. But your father is gone and your daughter is very much here. I *want* to help."

"You think I don't know that?" He nearly choked to keep his voice down. Brenda was jogging back down the sidewalk, waving something in her hand.

"Here you go," she said gaily, trotting up to them. She dropped the small box in Belle's hand.

"Thanks, Brenda. I'll replace this for you as soon as I can get over to the hardware store."

Brenda nodded. "Sure. Sure. Whenever." Her gaze bounced eagerly between Cage and Belle. "So, how is young Lucy doing? Such a terrible, terrible tragedy."

"Good grief, Brenda. Lucy's not paralyzed," Belle countered.

Brenda's smile stiffened. "Well, of course she isn't. And it's so nice of Cage to give you a job, too, after all that—" she waved her hand "—messiness you had in Cheyenne."

Save him from catty women. He took the box and pulled out the spark plug, kneeling down to replace it. "Isn't that your youngest crossing the street, Brenda?" He knew it was because she brought her trio of brats to every school meeting he'd ever had to attend.

She turned around. "Timothy Wyatt," she yelled, dashing after the boy. "You get out of the street this instant!"

"Nothing quiet about living down the street from the Wyatts," Belle murmured.

"Wouldn't think so." When the spark plug was in place, Cage rose. He primed the engine, then grabbed the cord and gave it one good pull. The engine turned over and ran, smooth as butter.

Belle's hands closed over the handle. "Thanks. I, um, well you should go on inside and wash your hands at least. So you don't get grease all over you the way I have."

Looking at her various splotches of grease only meant letting his gaze wander back to the vicinity of her bikini top. Not a good idea. He nodded and headed up the narrow, flower-lined walk while Belle busily pushed her mower over the postage-stamp-size lawn.

Inside, the house was small. Newer than his place, but much smaller, and that was saying something. When he'd come here to ask her in person to take the job, he'd stood on the little porch. Both times. He hadn't wanted to go inside her house any more than she'd been prepared to invite him inside.

He'd thought then, and he thought so now, that the small house was hardly the kind of place where he'd have expected Gus Day's daughter to live. The man had been the most prominent attorney in Cheyenne.

He went into the kitchen—a straight shot through the small living room—and washed up at the sink there. She had little pots of daisies sitting in the window next to a small round oak table. Photographs were stuck all over the refrigerator door with funky magnets.

He didn't particularly want to see all the mementos of her family. Her friends. He looked, anyway.

There were no photographs of her father that he could see. Just her with students he recognized from the school. With kids of all ages, many who were members of the Clay family. Several with a woman who looked a lot like Belle, except for their coloring. Probably the sister.

He leaned closer to one photo. Belle, grinning from ear to ear, a mortarboard on her head and a diploma clutched in her hand. She looked young and carefree. Not much different then she usually looked now.

He'd finally gotten his college degree when he'd been twenty-five. Five years ago now.

He straightened and headed back out, just as she was coming in. Bits of grass clung to the legs of her jeans and he stopped short when she suddenly leaned over, whipping them down her legs, kicking them free to leave on the porch. "Get the grease off?"

He was long past the teenage kid who'd been struck dumb by the seductive efforts of an older blonde, but right then Cage felt just as poleaxed by Belle as he'd been by his first experience with any woman. Only now he knew how high the cost could be.

"Cage?"

The rest of her bathing suit—cut like snug boxers—was modest by current standards. But it still showed enough.

She glanced down at herself, grimacing. "Sorry. I should have warned you." She walked past him to the kitchen.

He could probably span her waist with his two hands.

The swells of her breasts—the pink-tipped visions he wouldn't be getting out of his head anytime soon—would fit the palms of his hands. And her hips…

He heard the rush of water when she turned on the faucet and shifted sideways a little. He could see her vigorously scrubbing her hands and arms with soapy water. When she was done and dry, she grabbed a long-sleeved white shirt off the coat rack by the back door and slipped into it. The tails hung around her knees. It was obviously a man's shirt.

"Warned me?" Whose shirt was it?

"The scars. Well, you've seen a little of them already."

Right. Scars. They were there all right. But it wasn't the scars that had made his jeans so damn tight he could hardly move without making the problem obvious. "How long did it take you to recover?"

She flipped her ponytail free of the collar and padded into the living room, not looking at him.

Good thing.

"I'll let you know when I'm finished." She was leaning over, busily stacking together the magazines scattered over the top of the iron-and-glass coffee table. The shirt crept up the back of her insanely perfect thighs.

Was she doing it deliberately?

He ran his hand around his neck. He was driving Lucy down to visit his mother that afternoon. Even thinking about his daughter and his mother didn't alleviate the knot inside him.

Belle straightened and turned, her faint smile rueful. "Almost two years, actually. Recuperating put me behind a grade in junior high school. Hopefully, if we get Lucy's test scores high enough, she won't have to deal with being held back. I had to work with a tutor, too. In high school. All three years, to make up time. So my twin sister wouldn't graduate ahead of me."

He'd had enough reminders of her family. "Do you always strip off in front of strange men?"

Her dark lashes dipped for a moment, then she eyed him with wide eyes. "Why, yes, I do, Cage. I thought you knew that about me." She propped her hand on her hip, but her face was red. "And are you still going to keep calling me Miss Day even now that we know each other so well? Having seen me in my bathing suit, the way you have, that is. Why, we just might have to get married for the scandal of it all."

"You've got a smart mouth."

"The better to eat you with, Goldilocks," she muttered, turning away.

He nearly choked, but she was oblivious.

"I'm allergic to grass, okay? And my jeans were covered with it." She didn't look at him as she returned to the kitchen once more. Apparently, her bravado went only so far.

He followed. "Then why mow your own grass if you're allergic?"

"Well, who *else* would be doing it?"

"Hire someone."

She gave him a cross look. "I could say the same to you, then you would have some *time* to give to your daughter when she needs you. What *is* your real name, anyway?"

"What?"

"Cage isn't your real name, right?"

"No."

"Kind of an odd nickname."

"So?"

"So…how'd you get it? I'm sort of surprised it's not *rock,* because sometimes you act as if you're living under one."

"Calling me a snake?"

Her expression stilled for a moment. "No, actually. I've met one of *those.* Was engaged to him, actually."

Despite Cage's aversion to gossip, he'd heard the brunt of Belle's story. Was the former fiancé the owner of the shirt? Dammit. He didn't want to wonder. He damn sure refused to care.

"I paced," he said abruptly. Anything was better than thinking about how Belle came by the shirt she wore with such casual sexiness.

She looked blank.

"When I was a kid and indoors, I paced. Back and forth like I was in a cage."

"Ah." She yanked open the refrigerator and pulled out two longnecks. Extended one to him.

He shook his head.

"Seriously?"

"I don't drink."

She shrugged and put the beer back, then came out with bottles of water, instead. She handed him his, then leaned her shoulders against the fridge, opening her water. She tilted her head back and drank deeply, then capped the bottle again, resting it against her abdomen. "So, you like being outside better than inside, ergo, *Cage.* The pacing thing, by the way, seems to be something you got over. I've never seen a man who could be so still as you are. And you don't drink. What else is there about you that the Weaver grapevine hasn't already published? Ah. How ironic. Back to the beginning, again. Your real name."

"It's…unique." His voice was clipped. He strongly considered dumping the cold water over his head. Nearly anything would be preferable to the unacceptable thoughts running through his head.

Her eyebrows rose. "You're actually giving a hint? I'm amazed. Something unique. Unique for the English language? For a man? What?"

"Are you going to be at the Lazy-B tomorrow morning, or not?"

Her eyes narrowed in consideration. She tapped her finger against her water bottle, drawing his gaze for too long a moment. Then, her finger stilled midtap, and her cheeks colored, her gaze flicking to his, then away.

So, she wasn't as unaware as she'd seemed.

If it were anyone other than her, he'd do what nature intended. He'd step up to her, press her back flat against that photo-strewn refrigerator, kiss her until neither one of them knew their own names—real or nick—and tug away that bathing-suit top to see if her nipples tasted as sweet as he feared.

And she still hadn't given him an answer. "Miss Day?"

"One condition," she said after a moment.

"What?" He wasn't agreeing until he knew what sort of string she was dangling.

"Well, maybe more than one."

His molars were nearly grinding together. "What?"

"Not treating me like the enemy is probably more than I can expect. But you can at least stop acting like I'm some schoolmarm and call me *Belle*. You don't freak out if we visit…*visit*…the stable. *And* you suggest to Lucy that she have a birthday party."

"A party?" He eyed her. "Lucy doesn't want a party."

Belle *tsked.* "You may be able to spot a faulty spark plug, Cage, but *I* can recognize a lonely girl when I see one. Besides, she and I have talked about it. She wants a party but she figures you'll refuse to allow it."

"If she wants a party, fine."

"With boys?" Her eyebrows rose a little.

"What?"

"Loosen up, *Dad,*" she said evenly. "Your daughter is a teenager, and teenagers do generally have some interest in the opposite sex, if you can remember."

He remembered all right. He remembered where his thoughts had been when he'd been thirteen-fourteen-going-on twenty. "I remember what teenagers do with the opposite sex." Same damn thing he inconveniently thought of nearly every time he set eyes on *Miss* Belle Day. "I remember what I was doing when I was barely seventeen. Conceiving Lucy."

Belle's lashes lowered for a moment and when she looked up again, he knew that statement hadn't been some big revelation for her. Of course not. She may have lived in Weaver for only six months, but that would be long enough for a town where gossip vied with ranching as the number-one occupation. "I seriously doubt you were just out sowing your oats," she said after a moment. "Your dad had died. Your mom was critically injured. You had the responsibility of the ranch on your shoulders. You were alone, and you probably needed someone. Badly, I'd imagine."

He'd had responsibility for the ranch since he'd been

younger than that. "I had a hard-on for a sexy blonde I saw dancing at a rodeo," he said flatly. Understanding, sympathy or anything of that ilk were not things he wanted from Belle. "Fortunately, I've learned how to ignore wanting things that aren't good for me."

She flushed, obviously realizing where the pointed comment was directed. Too bad he could see the way that rosy color drifted down her throat, to her chest. Because it made him wonder how far the blush went.

She set aside the water bottle and clutched the shirt together with both hands. "Well. Anyway. Your daughter and her friends are more interested in holding hands and getting up the nerve to dance with a boy than…anything else. You agree and I'll be there tomorrow morning."

"She can have a party."

"And?" Her eyebrows rose expectantly.

His jaw felt tight. "You can visit the horses, but I'd appreciate it if you'd wait until I could be there, too." It was the most reasonable he could be.

She inclined her head. "And?"

And. Always another *and.* "And if I'd had a schoolmarm who looked like you, I wouldn't have been ditching classes to sleep with a wannabe dancer named Sandi Oldham." He reached out and brushed his thumb over her soft lips, watching her eyes flare. "Believe me, Miss Day. Some things are better left alone."

Chapter Seven

Belle's second drive out to the Lazy-B was accomplished without a deluge of rain.

Instead, she had to deal with a deluge of nervousness that put her misgivings on the first trip to shame.

The drive took much less time, courtesy of the dry roads, as well as her familiarity with the route. So, it wasn't even lunchtime when she closed the gate behind her and drove up to the brick house.

Strudel was again lying on the porch, but he popped up and scrambled down the steps to greet her when she climbed out of her Jeep. She laughed a little, scrubbing his neck as he jumped up on her. "What'd you eat this time that got you banished from the house?"

The dog panted and rolled his eyes in joy.

"Strudel." Cage's voice from the porch wasn't loud,

but the command was unmistakable. "Get off the woman."

The dog went back down on all fours. Danced around in circles. Belle ducked back into the Jeep to grab her suitcase. She felt some sympathy for the dog. There was enough adrenaline jolting through her system that she could have run in mindless circles, too.

She hadn't really expected to see Cage just yet. Running even a small ranch offered enough tasks to keep ten men busy, much less one. But he *was* there, and she'd have to suck it up. Just because she'd spent the rest of the previous day and night preoccupied with the things he'd said…the way he'd *looked* at her…

She realized she was still standing there with her rear hanging out of her old Jeep. Hardly conveying a composed demeanor. She yanked out the suitcase and closed the door. Cage had moved down the steps and was heading her way.

"Where's Lucy?" A nice touch of brightness in her voice. Not too shrill. Not too desperate. First order of business with the girl was to find out why she'd implied to her dad that Belle was prepared to quit.

"Talking to Anya on the phone about the birthday party. You were right."

Hallelujah. One good deed accomplished. Though she was surprised that he so easily acknowledged it. She hastily surrendered her suitcase when he reached for it. Easier than fighting over the thing.

He looked amused, as if he recognized her scrambled thoughts. A disturbing idea. She reached back inside her vehicle. "I nearly ran into the mailman on the road here," she said. "Thought I'd save you a trip."

If she hadn't imagined the glint of humor in those eyes that rivaled the sky for color, it disappeared when she held up the bundled newspaper and envelopes. He silently took the mail and turned back to the house.

Belle sighed at the slap of the wooden screen behind him. "Why, it was my pleasure, Cage. You're *so* welcome." She followed him up the steps where the ramp still blocked half the width. If she did her job well enough, he'd be able to dismantle it for good. Once inside the house, she heard Cage's footsteps overhead and knew he was putting her suitcase in her room.

Lucy was sprawled on her bed in her downstairs room, the phone apparently glued to her ear. She waved and smiled widely when Belle stuck her head through the doorway. She pressed the phone to her shoulder. "You're back!"

"Yes," Belle said arching her eyebrows. "Apparently, that's some big surprise."

The girl had the grace to look somewhat chagrined. "Well, now you know my dad really wants you."

Belle tucked her tongue between her teeth for a moment. She knew what Lucy meant, though the words suggested something quite different. "Finish your call," she suggested. "Then we'll get down to business."

Lucy grimaced. "You're not, like, going to take it out on me by making me do some really hideous exercises or something, are you?"

Belle smiled wickedly.

Lucy groaned. When Belle turned back to the staircase, she heard Lucy giggling into the phone again, though. Obviously, she wasn't too fearful of Belle's retribution.

She dashed up the staircase. Sure enough, Cage had put her suitcase on the foot of the bed, and she unpacked again, as quickly as she had the previous week. After all, her clothes took up no more space now than they had then.

She closed the door long enough to exchange her jeans for Capri tights that she covered with a loose pair of shorts, then put on her tennis shoes again and went back downstairs. Cage was in his office. She could see a wedge of his shoulder through the doorway.

Fortunately, the clump of Lucy's crutches coming along the wood floor put the kibosh on any notion she might have been entertaining of going toward that office. What would she have said, anyway?

They were who they were and never the twain would meet.

A shiver danced down her spine and she looked up at the ceiling. Maybe the place was developing a draft.

Right. Blame your nerves on phantom drafts. That's a sane thing to do.

"Belle?" Lucy was standing nearby watching her. "Something wrong?"

Belle shook her head. Then did a double take. "Good grief. You're wearing…blue."

"And you're wearing yellow. Call the newspapers. Come on. Just don't torture me too bad, okay?"

There were already filled water bottles in the refrigerator. Belle hid a smile at that. The prep work had to have been Lucy's doing, because she just couldn't envision Cage taking the time to fill water bottles. She grabbed two, and they walked outside, crossing to the barn. They'd only made it halfway when Strudel came tearing after them. He ran to the barn, then back, barking gleefully.

"That dog needs antidepressants," Belle said as she pushed open the barn door.

Lucy laughed. "Dad found him on the side of the highway last winter. He's a happy dog."

"So I see." It should have been harder to envision cranky Cage stopping to rescue some cold, shivering puppy. But it wasn't hard, and the image burned bright in her mind.

Then Lucy flipped on the boom box that Belle had left there. Debussy soared out, startling the images from Belle's head.

Good thing.

Belle dragged the blue mats into place, then Lucy dropped her crutches and inched to the floor, balancing her awkward position with no small amount of grace.

"You're going to dance on the stages of New York one day," Belle murmured. "Specially if you work as hard on your recovery as I know you can."

Lucy flushed. But she looked pleased by the idea. "My mom is a dancer. Did you know that?"

"Yes."

"That's why she's not here, you know. Because she went to Europe to be a dancer."

Belle knew what it was like to strive for a career, but privately, she couldn't imagine leaving behind her own child. "Do you hear from her?"

"I've got copies of programs from her shows," Lucy said, not exactly answering as she reclined again. She lifted her uninjured knee up to her chest, then slowly straightened it, her toes pointed, knee nearly resting on her nose.

A program was not a phone call or a letter, Belle thought. And because she was too curious about the role that Sandi Oldham played in the Buchanans' life, she kicked off her shoes.

"All right," she said briskly. "Let's get you warmed up. We have a lot to accomplish today. After we're done in here, you have a history test to pass."

Lucy groaned.

Standing just outside the barn door, Cage watched Belle and his daughter. Even Strudel sat quietly for once, leaning heavily against Cage's leg, occasionally slapping the dusty ground with his feathered tail. Lucy started out muttering and outright complaining about every single movement Belle put her through. But he never noticed a single sign of impatience in Belle. She was calm, encouraging, humorous. No matter what Lucy threw her way, she maneuvered his daughter into accomplishing whatever task she'd set out.

And eventually, Lucy was grinning as often as she was groaning.

Even though he had a million and one things that needed tending, Cage stayed there, out of sight, for the entire session. Only when Belle was helping Lucy get her leg situated in the whirlpool afterward did he finally turn away.

Belle might be a Day, she might be a pure source of frustration for his peace of mind, but where Lucy was concerned, Cage felt as if he'd finally done something right.

There was no way a judge could come along now and say that *anyone* could provide better for his own daughter.

Cage's satisfaction lasted well into the next week. And when it ended, it wasn't even because of Belle Day. It was because of his daughter.

He watched her from the door of his office. Watched her long enough to know she hadn't just gone in there for a piece of paper or some such thing. Not that he'd really believed it, given the fact it was nearly midnight.

He leaned his shoulder against the doorjamb. "Who were you calling?" His voice was mild, but she nearly jumped right out of her skin, casting him a guilty look that made his insides tighten.

"Nobody."

He pointedly looked at the telephone situated two inches away from her twitching fingers. "Is that their first or last name?"

She glared at him for a tense moment. Then her face crumpled and she burst into tears and snatched her crutches, racing past him. A few seconds later, she slammed her bedroom door behind her.

He let out an exasperated sigh. The kid had been moody as all get-out for days. He strode after her, only to find she'd locked the door. He rapped on it. "Luce. Unlock it."

"Leave me alone!"

"Who were you talking to on the phone?"

"I *said* leave me alone!" Her muffled voice rose.

He knocked harder. "Open the damn door."

"Cage?" Belle darted down the stairs, peering at him over the banister. "What's wrong?"

"Nothing that concerns you."

She straightened so fast her hair danced around the shoulders of her white robe. "Pardon me." She pivoted on the stairs, going up even faster than she'd come down. Which was saying something.

He jiggled the knob. "Unlock it, Luce, or I will."

The door yanked inward. Lucy glared at him. She was sitting in her chair. "I don't want to talk to *you*. I wanna talk to Belle."

Sixty-three inches of not-so-little girl knew how to pack a punch. He eyed her for a long moment. She eyed him right back. God help him, she was the spitting image of the woman who'd borne her, but he knew she got her attitude straight from him. "Who were you talking to on the phone?" If it was the Oldhams, he was going to have the bloody phone disconnected.

"I don't have to tell you!"

He lifted his eyebrow. "Oh?"

She exhaled loudly. If she could have managed it, he was pretty sure she would have stomped her feet. Instead, she wheeled her chair sharply away from the doorway. "I wanna talk to Belle." Her voice was thick with tears again.

He shoveled his fingers through his hair. "She's your physical therapist," he said flatly. "And it's the middle of the night."

"She's also my *friend*."

While he was only Lucy's dad. And no matter how much he needed to keep Belle Day firmly in one slot, she kept slipping out of it.

He watched Lucy surreptitiously swipe her cheeks. Dammit.

He went upstairs. Stared at another closed door for a long moment. Then knocked.

Belle opened it so fast, he wondered if she'd been standing there waiting for the opportunity to gloat. Only he couldn't detect any complacency in her expression. She just looked soft. From the top of her rippling brown hair to the tender toes peeking out beneath her long robe.

He was being punished for something, surely. Why else would he be surrounded by females he didn't know how to handle?

"Lucy wants to talk to you."

She tightened the belt of her robe, clearly hesitating.

"What are you waiting for? Yes or no?"

Her soft eyes cooled. "I'm waiting to see if you keel over, because I'm sure you must be choking on coming up here to pass that on."

"If you don't want to go down, say so."

"Given my continued presence under your roof each week, I'd think it would be clear by now that I'd do just about anything for Lucy."

"And nothing for me."

Her eyebrow rose and even though he could practically tuck her in his pocket, she managed to look down her nose at him. "As if you'd accept…anything." Her lips twisted a little and she planted her hand in the center of his chest, pushing until he moved out of the way.

When he did, she slid past him, a wisp nearly smothered in white terrycloth and topped by wavy brown hair.

He followed her downstairs. Told himself he imagined the oddly sympathetic look in her eyes in the moment before Lucy shut the door. Females on the inside.

Him on the outside.

He scrubbed his hand down his face and returned to his office. His desk was a jumble of papers, books and a hackamore he was repairing. The telephone sat smack in the middle of it all.

Who had she been calling? If it were just her friend, Anya, Luce would simply have told him. He'd have been irritated that she was up so late—and on a long-distance phone call, yet—but hardly enough to inspire that reaction. He rounded the desk and sat down. Leaned back in his chair.

Across from him, pinned to the wall, were all of Lucy's school photographs. But he didn't need the pictures to remember every single moment. The missing teeth. The crooked ponytails. The grins.

"Are you all right?"

His gaze slid to the doorway. Belle stood there. Arms crossed, hands disappearing up the opposite sleeves of her robe.

"She called the Oldhams, didn't she?"

Belle looked startled. "Her grandparents, you mean?"

"What did she tell you?"

"Don't bark at me. The only thing I know about her grandparents are that they've sent her some gifts. Dance programs of her mother's."

"Gifts including that horse." That horse that Belle insisted on letting Lucy visit. He'd gone with them once. Been frustrated as all hell to see that Belle had been right about something else. Lucy might talk a fast game about wanting back on Satin, but she was definitely afraid.

He looked up at Belle, sidetracked a little by the gleam on her lips when she moistened them. "Yes," she admitted. "Lucy...mentioned it."

He propped his elbows on his desk, crinkling letters and invoices. "Then what *did* she tell you?"

She looked down the hallway for a moment then stepped more fully into the confines of his office. There was no chair for her to sit. "She didn't tell me she'd called her grandparents tonight."

Which didn't mean that Lucy hadn't made the call. She thought he didn't know about the other times she'd called. "Then what's she going on about?" Having to voice the question stuck in his craw big-time.

"We, um, we need to go into town tomorrow."

"For cake mix and candles already?"

Her cheeks were pink. "Well. We could do that."

"I find it hard to believe she's going berserk at midnight over a cake she doesn't even need for weeks yet. It's not like she's going to be troubled over picking a color for the frosting. It'll be pink. Or pink."

"She's not upset about her cake."

"Then what?" He pushed away from his desk only there was no room to pace in the small room. Not unless he wanted to go near Belle, and he didn't want to do that.

Because getting *near* wasn't remotely as close as he wanted to be. And knowing it just pissed him off even more.

"There's something else you need to know." Belle was looking anywhere but at him. "Lucy didn't even want to tell you, but I said she really needed to."

His neck tightened warningly. "What?" His voice was harsh and Belle took a step back.

"Nothing bad," she assured quickly.

"Nothing bad that has her sneaking in my office to use the phone when she's supposed to be sleeping? If she wasn't calling her grandparents, who the hell was she calling?"

"Evan Taggart."

He stared. "What?"

"Who," Belle murmured. "But she didn't get hold of him, anyway, because his parents answered the phone and said it was too late to talk."

"At least Drew Taggart has some sense," he muttered. "So she was upset because she couldn't talk to some little kid."

"Evan's in her grade, Cage. She…likes…him. I think the Taggarts have been out of town on vacation or something. She was making sure he knew he was invited to her party."

He absorbed that.

"But that's not the real problem."

"Then what the hell is?"

"Would you calm down?" She moistened her lips. "Seriously, this is nothing for you to be wigging out over and—"

He grabbed her shoulders. "What…is…it?"

Her lashes lowered. "Well, actually, Lucy got her first period tonight. She's too embarrassed to tell you. And that's why we need to go to town tomorrow. Because I wasn't exactly prepared for this, either."

He sat down on the edge of his desk. "What?"

She tugged her belt tighter. "Judging by your expression, I think you heard me just fine."

"She's only twelve!"

Belle quickly pushed his office door closed even though she knew the barrier wouldn't completely buffer Cage's raised voice. "You want to argue Mother Nature with me? She's all but thirteen, and regardless of *what* her age is, this is happening." She almost felt sorry for him. He looked positively shell-shocked. But sympathy didn't quite douse the sting of being put in her place by him.

"Your daughter is growing up, Cage, and you better start getting used to the idea, or you're going to be dealing with a lot of episodes just as pleasant as this one! The poor thing is being ruled by hormones right now."

He was silent for a moment. Then he held out his hands, cupped palms turned upward. "When she was born I could hold her right here in the palms of my hands. She was that small." His fingers curled and he dropped his fists. "Lucy's always been able to talk to me."

So much for holding on to her indignation.

She impulsively caught his hands in hers, smoothing out his fingers from those tense fists. "This isn't about you, Cage. It's about her. She's no more used to the things that are going on inside her—emotionally and physically—than you are."

His lashes lifted and his eyes met hers. She was abruptly aware that holding his hands wasn't just a matter of trying to extend comfort.

It felt intimate.

It felt addictive.

She started to pull away. But his thumbs pressed over her fingertips, holding them in place. She could feel the calloused ridges as he slowly brushed over her fingers, grazing over her knuckles.

Her lips parted, yet her breathing had stalled.

They were so close she could easily pick out the black ring surrounding his blue, blue irises. Could have counted each black lash that comprised the thick smudged-coal lashes he'd passed on to his daughter. Could have touched the nearly invisible scar on his chin just below the curve of his lower lip.

She realized she was leaning in, and shock jerked her back, hands and eyes and traitorous hormones and all. Was she no better than Annette Barrone?

He wrapped his hands around the edge of his desk on either side of his hips. "Put whatever you need in town on my account," he said after a moment. His voice was low.

She nodded and starting backing out of the office. Bumped into the door that she'd closed. Heat stung her cheeks as she fumbled for the knob. Thankfully, the door opened. Escape was near.

"Belle."

She really felt safer when he called her *Miss Day*. Did he know how close she'd come to leaning forward those last few inches and pressing her lips to his? "Yes?" Lord, she hoped not. Her humiliation would be complete.

"Thank you."

Her knees threatened to dissolve right there. She nodded quickly and poured herself out of his office.

She hoped to heaven that he couldn't see the way she had to wait until she stopped shaking at the foot of the stairs before climbing them. She hoped to heaven that when she did go up the stairs, she'd remember somewhere along the way that Cage Buchanan was off limits.

He blamed her father for the accident that stole his parents. He didn't know—couldn't possibly—that it was Belle's fault that she and her father had been out at all on that icy road that long-ago night.

Chapter Eight

Cage saw her coming. There was no mistaking the sheaf of brown hair streaming back from her as she leaned low over the horse, seeming to race with the wind. Belle was quite a sight. Three weeks had passed since that night in his office. Three weeks of relative peace and quiet. Except for the nights, spent wakeful and alert with her only a room away.

He propped his wrists over the end of the posthole digger and watched her closing the distance between them. Anticipation tangled with wariness and it wasn't a combination he particularly welcomed.

At least she wasn't foolish enough to be riding that satanic horse. No matter how well Lucy was doing after working with Belle all this time, he'd have still probably fired Belle for it.

The horse was a line he wouldn't let anyone cross.

He leaned the digger against the truck and shoved his wire clippers back in his toolbox, then sat on the opened tailgate and chugged down a half a bottle of water, waiting.

Because sure as God made little green apples, he knew that Belle Day was gunning for him.

He heard the hooves pound and wouldn't allow himself the luxury of looking away as she neared, slowly reining in the animal. She looked fragile as she dismounted, but he knew only too well that she was nothing but muscle and nerve under those body-skimming clothes she wore.

She flipped the reins around the side-view mirror of the truck then lifted her hand, shading her eyes from the noonday sun as she looked at him. "As usual, you're a hard man to track down. Gone before breakfast. Back after dinner."

"Where's Lucy?"

"Emmy Johannson brought Anya out to visit now that she's back from visiting her father. They're eating lunch right now. Emmy's going to give Lucy a piano lesson, too."

"Then what's wrong?" He pulled a fence post out of the truck bed and shoved it into the hole he'd already dug, then pushed at it with his boot, aligning it. "And why didn't you drive?"

She propped her hands on her narrow hips and tilted her head. Her long hair flowed over her shoulder and her eyes glanced at him, then away. It had been that way for days. Weeks. Looking, but not looking.

Wanting but not touching. At least on his part, anyhow.

He kicked the post again.

"I'm not unfamiliar with horses," she countered. "I've been riding all my life. And I wasn't foolish enough to ride Satin. Though I did notice you're letting him run at least."

He hated the horse because of what he stood for and how it had hurt his daughter. But he wasn't cruel enough to keep the animal penned in a stall forever. He pushed the post once more, still not satisfied with the way it stood. "I'd have preferred you ask me, first."

She huffed a little then walked around him. "Fine. I will, next time." She grabbed the heavy post beneath his hands and put her shoulder against it, nudging it in his direction. "Centered?"

He narrowed his eyes, studying the top of her dark head for a moment. "Yeah." He made quick work out of filling the hole again then quickly fastened the barbed wire back in place when she moved out of the way.

She flipped her long ponytail behind her shoulders and pulled a long, thin envelope out from behind her. He barely glanced at the envelope, distracted by the wedge of skin she displayed when she'd flipped up her shirt to pull out the envelope tucked against her spine beneath it. "This looked important. A courier brought it out."

His stomach clenched as she extended the envelope.

He slowly took it. Eyed the embossed return address.

"Do you want to talk about it?" Her voice was surprisingly diffident.

"No." He folded the envelope in half then pushed it in his back pocket. If he had to read a letter that he was another step closer to losing custody of his baby, he damn sure didn't want to do it while Belle Day was standing there to witness it.

But she just stood there, though, hands clutched together. "Is there anything I can do?"

"No." Not unless she had about fifty grand lying around unused. He figured it would cost at least that much to get Sandi to back off. Either the money would go in her pocket, or the lawyer's. He turned back to the truck. Hoisted the next pole over his shoulder and moved down to the next hole.

"Cage, if you have some legal problem, my family might—"

"No." He didn't like feeling as if he'd kicked a calf when she paled a little and pressed her soft lips together. But he didn't have it in him just then to apologize.

"Well, then do you think—"

"Dammit to hell, Belle, I said no."

She winced. "You don't even know what I was going to ask!"

He exhaled roughly. Shoved the post into the ground with a vengeance. "I don't want your help. God knows I don't want your family's help. I don't want anything." Except her body. A problem which was becoming more evident by the minute. "Satisfied?"

"The Clays are having a party," she said stiffly. "They wanted me to extend the invitation to you and Lucy."

He looked up into the sky. He'd never had much against Squire Clay or his sons. The boys had been ahead of him a few years, but they knew each other passably. Didn't mean he wanted to sit down with tea and cookies across the table from Squire's wife, Gloria Day.

There was probably a special place in Hades for him, but he just couldn't look at the woman without thinking about his own mother, and what Gloria's husband had done to her. Call him a miserable puke, but there it was.

"What's the party for?"

Her brown eyes widened a little. Surprised that he'd bothered to ask, no doubt. "Angeline's birthday. She's Daniel and Maggie's oldest. The party is a week after Lucy's, actually."

He'd seen the girl. Dusky skinned. Pretty as a picture. All he knew about her was that her natural parents were dead and Daniel and Maggie had adopted her a long time ago. "Take Lucy."

"Really?"

He *really* wished she'd go on her way. The letter was burning a hole in his butt. "If she wants to go."

"Well." She brushed her hands together, obviously surprised. "This is wonderful. We'll be swimming. The Double-C has a great swimming hole, you see, and—"

"—and I don't have time to stand around shooting the breeze," he said flatly. "So why don't you go back and tend to what I *am* paying you for?"

Her chin lifted a little. "Keep up with the ogre routine, Cage. One of these days you'll have it perfected and maybe even you will forget it's an act." She strode over to the truck and snatched the reins. With a move he admired whether he wanted to or not, she slid onto the horse's back. In a flash, they were racing away.

When she was out of sight, he let his eyes rove over the land around him. When he'd inherited it, the Lazy-B hadn't been much more than a chunk of dirt from which his father had scratched out a meager living.

Now, it was prime. As was his stock. Prime enough that he knew he could get a decent price if he asked. God knew, he'd gotten more than a few offers over the years, specially from the Clays who ran the biggest operation in the entire state.

Problem was, Cage didn't want to sell.

But he didn't want to lose his daughter more.

He pulled out the letter and looked at the envelope. Delivered by a courier this time. Was that a polite word for a process server? He didn't know.

He went over to the truck. Sat down on the ground beside it in the shade and was glad there was no one but the birds sailing overhead to know his hands were shaking as he tore open the envelope.

The letter was brief. The missive unmistakable.

Sandi hadn't been bluffing. The Oldhams wanted Lucy in their family fold. And Sandi was using her parents' significant wealth to make it happen. He hadn't buckled to her, so she'd sicced her parents on him instead. And now their personal requests to see their granddaughter—denied by him—had become a legal challenge. For custody.

He leaned his head back against the truck and closed his eyes. And there was no way the attorney he'd been able to afford would be up to fighting the half-dozen attorneys the Oldhams had pitted against him. Even if he sold the ranch to pay an attorney of that caliber, there was little chance he'd win.

They were the Oldhams of Chicago. Bank president. Society matron. Old money, older reputation. Everything that Sandi had shunned when she'd been twenty years old. Everything she'd warned him about when she'd convinced him that telling her parents she was pregnant would be their biggest mistake. And back then he'd been more interested in keeping Sandi from doing something stupid to end her pregnancy than to argue the issue of informing *her* parents about the baby.

Obviously, it suited Sandi now to have her parents on her side. He pinched the bridge of his nose, fleeting ideas of taking his daughter and getting the hell out of Dodge hovering in his mind.

But he'd never been a runner. If he had been, he'd have run hard and fast from the responsibilities of a ranch and a child when he'd still been pretty much a kid himself.

He thumped his head back against the truck.

Lucy deserved more. She deserved every single privilege that came with being the only Oldham grandchild.

But lying down without a fight just wasn't something he could do.

"Cage?"

He pushed to his feet and pushed the papers into the envelope as he looked across the truck. Belle was back and he'd been too preoccupied to hear. "What?" He slammed down the lid of the toolbox, the envelope safely inside. If she asked him again about it, he was going to rip something apart.

Her hand was shading her eyes. "What were you doing? Hiding?"

No matter what, the idea had appeal. Take Lucy. Hide. Try and forget the turmoil caused by various members of the Day family. "Forget something?" She couldn't have made it to the house and all the way back again in the amount of time that had passed.

She slid off Dexter's back and tied him loosely,

again, to the truck's side mirror. "Figured Lucy wouldn't be finished with her lesson yet. And she needs some time to just hang with Anya, anyway. Are there more gloves in that toolbox?"

"Why?"

She shrugged and walked to the truck bed herself. "Because I don't want to get blisters."

He stepped in her path before she could flip open the toolbox. "Caused by…what?"

She pointedly looked at the posts stacked length-wise in the bed.

"I don't want your help." Her body? That was something entirely different.

God. He needed to get out of Weaver more often. There were plenty of women he knew around the state who were more than happy to spend a few recreational hours with him. Women who didn't want or expect anything more than what he was willing to share. Intelligent, independent, warm women, who never thought to—or wanted to—interfere in his life.

"Yes. You've made that abundantly clear," Belle said evenly. "The gloves?"

He frowned down at her, but she didn't come close to taking the hint. She just looked up at him, head tilted to one side, eyes squinting in the sunlight that turned her dark brown eyes to amber-stained glass. "You need a hat," he muttered.

"Well, it so happens that I don't have one of those, either." She lifted her shoulder, barely covered by the narrow strap of a snug gray shirt. "Just so you know, if I *do* get blisters, it's going to be hard for me to work out Lucy's muscle spasms, but—"

He nudged her aside and flipped up the toolbox, blindly grabbing a pair of leather gloves. He slammed the lid back down and slapped them in her hand. Then shoved his own bloody hat onto her head. "You're a pain in the ass, you know that?"

"I believe you've expressed that sentiment, as well, even if you haven't used those particular words." She nudged back the hat so it wasn't covering her eyes. It was too big for her.

But damned if she didn't look cute.

Bloody hell.

He yanked on his own gloves and reached for the posthole digger. Pushed it at her. "Know how to use one of those?" Maybe it would shut her up. Keep her from looking at him with those big brown eyes.

She rolled her eyes. A habit picked up from Lucy? "Yes," she drawled.

About as well as she knew how to fix her lawn mower, he figured. He shouldered a heavy post and headed away from the truck. She hurried after him. Five minutes, he calculated, and she'd be all too ready to go back to the sanctuary of the house.

Only five minutes passed and she showed no sign of stopping. Even though the ground was harder than stone and the muscles in her arms were standing out as she struggled.

He swiped his sweaty forehead with his arm. "Give me that."

"I can do it." Her voice was gritty.

"Maybe," he allowed blandly, "but why would you want to?"

She tossed her head, her tied-back hair rippling.

"God only knows," she muttered. She wrapped her fingers freshly around the long wooden handles. "Maybe because I still haven't gotten over needing to prove that I can." She lifted the digger and slammed it back into the earth. The sharp edges of the shovel finally bit. "Ha!" She pulled apart the handles, catching a small amount of dirt between the blades, then dropped it to one side.

There was such satisfaction in her sudden grin that Cage stepped back and let her work. Sweat was dripping from her forehead by the time she'd dug the hole deep enough for the post and tossed aside the digger.

"You gonna plant the post, too?" His voice was dry.

She shook her head, leaning over, arms braced on her thighs. "Wouldn't want you to start feeling wimpy," she said breathlessly. "Oh, God. Now that's some serious work, isn't it? No wonder you never have to touch the weights in the barn." She straightened, only to tear off her shirt and wipe her face with it.

He nearly swallowed his tongue, though the sport bra she wore was made of some thick gray stuff that was about as erotic as wool socks.

He had an unbidden vision of Belle wearing nothing *but* wool socks.

He shoved the post in place, backfilling the hole. "Now that you've played at manual labor, mebbe you could get back to your *real* work?" And leave him alone with his frustrating visions, fueled by the memory that wouldn't die even after all this time of her perfectly formed breasts.

She pulled off his cowboy hat and lifted her hair from her neck, stretching a little. "Everybody needs to play now and then," she said, her eyes slanting toward him. "Even you."

He grunted and turned away from the post. More importantly, he turned away from the sight of her, stretching like some sort of lithe cat. "Consider this my back nine."

"Do you golf?"

He looked at her.

Her lips twisted ruefully. "Suppose it's hard to golf, when there's no course around here."

"Suppose it's hard to golf when there's no time," he corrected.

"Do you even *know* how to play golf?"

"Do you?"

She shook her head.

He smiled a little despite himself and headed for the truck. Dexter had his nose buried in the grass, and didn't even lift his head when Cage passed him.

"You didn't answer." Belle said, following him.

"Observant of you."

"Afraid I might bandy about the news of your golfing prowess around Weaver?"

He spotted the tool chest in his truck bed and the brief spate of humor shriveled.

"Go back to the house, Miss Day," he said flatly, and plucked his hat out of her fingers. "Playtime is over."

She blinked a little. "Maybe if you *indulged* in some playtime, you'd start sleeping at night." She grabbed up Dexter's reins and smoothly swung up into the saddle.

As she rode away, he thought he heard her mutter. "Ogre."

Chapter Nine

"Range of motion remains severely limited despite marked increase in muscle tone and—" Belle stopped writing when she heard the scream.

Another nightmare. The third since the afternoon Belle had ridden out to see Cage.

She pushed back from the kitchen chair, concern propelling her down the hall even though she knew in her head that Cage would beat her to Lucy's room. Sure enough, he was striding into his old bedroom, and in the half light, she watched him sit on the side of Lucy's bed.

She hovered there for a moment, then turned back to the kitchen and her notes. She sat down, staring at the report that she made out each week charting Lucy's progress. But her mind was still stuck on the picture of Cage with his daughter.

She'd seen him helping Lucy with her exercises a

few days earlier. And had hidden out of sight, so as not to interrupt the moment. And, maybe, to absorb the knot of emotion the sight had caused inside her.

She pressed her lips together now, as unsettled as she had been then, and hurriedly shut the file folder.

She needed to talk to her sister. She and Nikki had been missing each other's phone calls for too many days now.

Her cell phone was upstairs in her room, but when she headed for the stairs, the sight of Cage standing in Lucy's doorway stopped her in her tracks.

"She's asking for you."

Belle paused, trying to read his expression. Should she refuse? Make some attempt at sliding back into the professional role she was supposed to be occupying?

She nodded silently and headed toward Lucy's room. Who was she trying to kid? Her professionalism where this family was concerned was nonexistent.

She slipped past Cage into the bedroom, casting him a quick look.

His face was hard.

She ducked her head again and crossed over to Lucy's bed, sitting in the same spot that Cage had. Lucy's hair was tumbled, her face glistening with sweat. Belle snatched a tissue from the box on the nightstand and pressed it to Lucy's forehead. "What's wrong?" Lucy shifted, looking past Belle.

She looked back to see Cage watching from the hall. At their attention, he turned on his heel and went into his office. The door shut after him.

Softly, quietly. Controlled.

Belle chewed the inside of her lip and focused once

more on Lucy. "Are you sick or something?" They'd already survived last month's first-period episode. Lucy, fortunately, had adjusted quickly enough.

Belle wasn't sure she could say the same of Lucy's father.

"I have a charley horse in my leg."

"Same place as before?" If the nightmares were frequent, the muscle spasms were more so. Nearly every day the girl had been plagued with muscle spasms in her calf. Lucy nodded and Belle pushed aside the bedding, reaching for Lucy's leg. She gently began massaging, and determined immediately that if Lucy'd *had* a charley horse, it was long gone. She kept working her fingers into the muscle, though. "Another bad dream?"

Lucy made a noncommittal sound, remembering to offer a wince now and then in honor of her phantom cramp.

"Want to talk about it?"

Lucy merely turned her cheek into her pillow.

"I used to have a recurring nightmare." Belle shifted so she was sitting more comfortably, and continued working Lucy's leg. "From when I was hurt."

"In the accident where my Grandma was hurt?"

"Yes."

"It was pretty bad, huh."

It took no effort at all for Belle to recall the excruciating details. Which she didn't want to do. "Yes. Anyway, I was in the hospital for weeks, too. Like you were after Satin threw you. Fortunately, I didn't need surgery like you did."

"How old were you?"

"Thirteen. I had nightmares for a long time after that."

Lucy's face was a canvas of shadows.

"I didn't dream about the accident, though. I kept dreaming that everyone I knew and cared about was walking. On a street, in a store. The places changed sometimes. But they were walking. And I couldn't keep up. Couldn't make myself take one single step no matter how hard I tried. I couldn't run, much less walk, after them. I couldn't walk *with* them." Her fingers slowed. "Of course, when I was awake, I knew that my family and my friends weren't leaving me behind, but when I was asleep?" She shook her head.

"But they stopped. The nightmares. Right?"

"Yes, they stopped."

Lucy looked at her. "When?"

"When I started talking about them." She waited a moment, hoping Lucy would heed the hint. But the girl remained silent. "Charley horse gone now?"

Lucy nodded.

"Good." She tucked the covers back in place and headed for the door. "G'night, sweetie."

"Belle? Could you—"

She stepped back to the bedside. "Could I what?" she prompted gently.

"StayuntilIgotosleep?" The words came out in a rush.

Belle's heart squeezed. "You bet." She pulled up the small pink chair that was crammed in the corner and sat beside the bed.

Lucy scooted further down her pillow and turned on her side, facing Belle. "Are you going to be here for my birthday party?" Her voice was little more than a whisper.

"If you want me to be."

Lucy nodded. She closed her eyes.

In minutes, she was asleep again.

Belle sat there a while longer, her thoughts tangled. When it seemed clear that Lucy was sleeping soundly, she quietly moved the chair back to the corner and left the room, pulling the door partially closed.

Cage's office, when she peeked around the doorway, was empty. But she didn't have to look far to find him. It was the middle of the night. Naturally, he would be sitting out on the porch, his long legs stretched out in front of him, his eyes staring into the dark.

She pushed open the screen to see him more clearly, but didn't go out. "Lucy's asleep again." Her heart ached a little, because she knew it had to sting that his daughter had turned to her again. "It's not my imagination that her nightmares are coming more often, is it?"

The shake of his head was slow in coming.

"Have you—" Lord, she didn't want him berating her for being interfering again "—um, have you told her physician that she's plagued with them?"

His gaze slid her way. Unreadable. He nodded. Shifted, crossing his boots at the ankle. The pose ought to have been casual. Relaxed.

Belle knew better. She also knew better than to probe for the reasons causing *his* habitual sleeplessness.

"She also asked if I'd stick around for her birthday party." Better to get that out now. The party was scheduled for Friday night, after Belle would have ordinarily left for the weekend.

"Damn straight," he murmured. "It was your idea in the first place. Least you can do is play chaperone."

She absorbed that, alternately glad that she wasn't going to have to butt heads with him over the matter, and unnerved that she didn't.

"Then you can kiss her wounds when the party is a bust," he added darkly.

"It's not going to be a bust."

"There's no room for a bunch of kids in this house."

"We'll figure it out. Maybe use the barn."

He shot her a look.

"I'm serious. Crepe-paper streamers and balloons. Plenty of soda and munchies. It'll be fine. In fact, it was Lucy's idea. She mentioned it earlier this week. We've already bought the decorations and stuff. We'll just put it all up in the barn instead of the house."

Cage ran his hand through his hair, finally showing some emotion. Chagrin. "Might as well. *This* place is a mess."

Belle chewed the inside of her lip. She was not going to be charmed by the dusky color running under his sharp cheekbones. If he hadn't been so ornery about her helping with some of the household tasks, the house *wouldn't* be quite as unkempt as it was. "Hard for one person to do everything," she said pointedly. Running the B. Raising a daughter on his own. Taking care of their sturdy, little brick home.

Cage hadn't responded—either to agree or disagree. And standing there in the doorway was making her feel out of place. She started to turn back inside.

"What if nobody comes?"

His gruff comment jangled in her head for a tight moment before her brain engaged her tongue. Instead of stepping inside, she stepped outside the screen door, her fingers holding the door long enough to let it close without a sound. "That won't happen, Cage," she assured quietly. "They are Lucy's friends."

"Their parents aren't mine."

She swallowed, pressing her lips together for a moment. She watched the bevy of moths beat themselves against the glow of the porch light. "Only because you won't let them be. The only reason people speculate so much about you is because you hold yourself apart from them."

"I don't like everyone knowing my business."

"This is a small community. That's bound to happen no matter what you like or don't like. And if you weren't so…standoffish—" She waited a beat at that, sure he'd cut her off. But he didn't. "Maybe people would surprise you. Maybe they'd accept your need for privacy more if you were more accepting of them." Which, even to her, sounded convoluted.

Disregarding the wisdom she was not displaying, she crossed the porch and sat on the low rail, facing him. The night air was cool on her bare arms but she knew if she went in for a sweater, the moment would be lost. "In any case, despite the fact that you hold others at a distance, Lucy hasn't. People in Weaver care about what happens to her, and they'll want to celebrate with her, too. Everyone who was invited accepted weeks ago. You can't really think that they'd blow her off now right before the party."

He looked far from convinced. "It's late. You should be in bed."

Her cheeks warmed, despite the cool night air. "You get up even earlier than I do. I don't know how you do it, frankly. I was still up so I could finish my report and get it in the mail to Lucy's orthopedist. Otherwise I'd be sawing logs by now."

"Lucky you." He leaned his head back against the chair, watching her from beneath lowered lids. "Did she tell you what her nightmare is about?"

Those thin slices of blue—pale even in the subdued porch light—were unsettling and she looked down at her stockinged feet. Two inches from his boots.

She curled her toes down against the wood porch and shook her head. "She'll talk when she's ready, I imagine. Same way she puts effort into her therapy only when she's ready."

"She's been doing her exercises on her own on the weekends."

"I know. I can tell when we work together each Monday. She's still not making the progress I would have hoped." Belle wasn't sure what made her admit that to him. It wasn't that Lucy wasn't progressing at all.

"And what did you hope for? To have her dancing on her tocs by Thanksgiving?" He sat forward suddenly, elbows on knees, fingers raking through his hair.

If she lifted her hand, she'd be touching the bronzed strands springing back from his forehead. She pressed her fingertips harder against the wooden rail beneath her. "Maybe not by Thanksgiving," she admitted. "Now, Christmas?" She shrugged, smiling a little, even though they both knew Belle would be long gone before either holiday.

"She's on crutches. Not walking on her own entirely, but given what the doctor told us after the accident— that she might not walk that well again, ever—I think it's pretty amazing." Then he glanced up at her, the corners of his lips turning up.

The surprise of that half smile had her nearly falling backward off the rail. She jerked a little and he shot out his hand, grabbing hers. "Thanks." She hoped he'd blame her breathlessness on being startled.

"I don't need you breaking your neck on top of everything else," he muttered.

So much for him nearly smiling. She wiggled her fingers, drawing attention to his continued hold and he released her.

Her wrists still felt surrounded by a ring of warmth as she scooted past him toward the door. Asking him what caused *his* sleeplessness would be pointless. Foolish.

She still wondered.

A lot.

She opened the door and quickly went inside. "Good night, Cage."

Not until she was nearly at the foot of the staircase did she hear his quiet reply. "Good night, Belle."

She tightened her grip on the banister and forced her feet to the first riser. And the next. It was frightening how hard it was to continue when everything inside her was tugging on her to go back out there. To keep poking and prodding as if *she* could break through his barriers.

Crazy. That's what she was.

She passed Cage's room, carefully averting her eyes from looking inside, and went in her own room. She'd barely climbed into bed—which had been squeaking again for a solid month despite Cage's efforts shortly after she'd arrived—when her cell phone gave a soft squawk.

She grabbed it off the nightstand. "Nik?"

"I've been calling you for hours."

Something inside her went on full alert. "What's wrong?"

"Who said anything's wrong?" Nikki's voice was tight. "I've left you a half-dozen messages."

Belle flopped on her back, covering her eyes with her hand. "I'm sorry. I should have tried harder to reach you. Oh, God, Nik. I don't know what I'm doing here. Why I thought I could…make up somehow for the past."

"Scott's been released."

Her thoughts floundered. "What? Oh. Well, good. Then his wife won't be making the staff there miserable."

Nikki was silent for a long moment. "Okay, catch me up here, Belle. When you said make up for the past, I thought you meant proving to yourself that you had what it took to be a good therapist. After Scott blamed you because he wasn't ever going to be able to get back to football—"

"Scott hasn't even been the last thing on my mind," she murmured truthfully. And it was a relief to know it. "I wanted…I very nearly…I wanted to kiss him, Nikki. Taste him. Breathe him in. More than once now."

"Scott…oh, no." Dismay colored her sister's voice. "Please tell me you're not talking about Cage Buchanan."

"Okay, I'll tell you that," Belle whispered after a long moment. "But I'd be lying." She waited for Nikki to say all the things that were running through her own mind.

Don't get personally involved with patients or their families.

Don't get personally involved with a man who loathes your parentage.

Don't get personally involved period, end of story.

Nikki said none of them. She merely sighed. "Oh, Belle."

And with that soft, sympathetic murmur, tears stung Belle's eyes. "He's a good man, Nik. And he loves his daughter so much it is heartbreaking and beautiful all at the same time."

"What are you going to do about it?"

Her fingers plucked at the quilt. Had Cage's mother made it? Was quilting just one more thing that had been amputated from her existence the night of the car accident? "There's nothing *to* do. He didn't hire me out of personal interest, after all." Far from it. "I'm here because of Lucy. I just need to focus on her and everything will be fine."

The words rang a little too hollow, and Belle was grateful that her sister refrained from observing it. "So, why the half-dozen messages to call you back, anyway?"

"I quit."

The words made no sense at first. "What? Oh, hell's bells." She sat forward on the bed, pressing the phone tighter to her ear. "Why? Alex refused to give you the raise you deserve, didn't he? Is he out of his tiny little mind?"

"I never asked for the raise." Nikki's voice sounded

thick and Belle realized her sister had been crying. She felt like a selfish witch for not having immediately noticed.

"Then why? You love your job." She heard Nikki sigh shakily and her nerves tightened. "Nik? What's really going on here?"

"This is harder to tell than I thought it would be."

"Nikki, you're scaring me. What?"

"I'm…um…I'm pregnant."

Belle blinked, staring blindly at her fingers that were clenching a handful of quilt.

"Belle?"

She scrambled. "Since when? Are you feeling okay? Have you been to the doctor?"

"Almost six weeks ago. Yes. And yes."

"Six weeks…God, Nik, I didn't even know you were involved with someone."

Her sister made a watery sound. "Well, that's just it, isn't it. I'm *not* involved."

"Then how—"

"The usual way."

Belle swallowed. Her sister didn't indulge in casual sex any more than Belle did. "I'm coming down to see you."

"No. You have a job there."

"Then I'll come on the weekend. Don't try to put me off, Nicole. I'm not going to rest until I've seen you in person. Have you told Mom?"

"No. And you better not, either."

"She's going to have to know sooner or later. Angel's party is a week from Saturday. You're going to the ranch for it, aren't you? Mom's going to know something is up."

"I'll deal with next week…next week. Look, Belle. We're not sixteen years old anymore. I just…need some time before I tell her."

Belle chewed her lip. Her sister had always been the one with straight As in school. Who'd never taken a single step off the line of excellence and responsibility. It was Belle who'd been the one to bumble through life. Not Nikki. "What about the father?" She pushed at her temples. "And why quit your job now? You're going to need your medical benefits…unless, do you already have someplace else you're going to?"

"No."

"Then why quit? I can't believe Alex let you go after all this time. Does he know? Is that why he allowed you to leave? There are laws, Nikki—"

"The only one who knows is you. I needed to tell someone or I was going to go mad."

"I have a million questions, you know."

"I know. Can we just deal with them another day?"

"Yes." Her sister was pregnant. And Belle hadn't felt a hint of it. "You're sure you're feeling okay?"

"Tired. Otherwise, fine."

"And you're done talking for now," Belle surmised.

"Yes."

Her eyes stung. "I love you, you know. No matter what goes on. You're going to be a great mother."

Nikki's soft laugh was watery, but it was a laugh. "You'll be a great aunt."

"I'm coming down this weekend," Belle reminded, half warning, half reassuring.

"G'night, Annabelle." Her sister hung up.

Belle stared at the small phone in her hand for a moment, then tossed it aside. She pushed off the bed, and left the room, her mind too busy to rest.

The house was dark now, Cage's bedroom door closed. She let herself out the kitchen door and was halfway to the barn before she realized she hadn't put on her shoes. Her soles prickled, but she didn't turn back.

Inside the barn, she blindly stuck a CD in the sound system, turned it down from Lucy's preferred roar, and dragged out a floor mat. An hour later, she was still at it. Two hours later, her muscles were screaming and her hair was clinging to her sweaty face and neck. Her mind was still teeming, but at least she'd managed to numb the questions into submission. She blew out a long breath and dropped down onto the incline bench, closing her eyes.

Maybe she'd just sleep right there.

"Get 'em worked out?"

Numb enough not to be startled when Cage spoke. She looked at him. "What?"

"The demons," he said.

Not in a dozen workouts. "I thought you'd finally gone to bed." Maybe he had. He wore an untucked white T-shirt now with his jeans, instead of the chambray shirt from before. "Don't you *ever* sleep?"

He ambled closer. Handed her a small towel off the stack she'd kept handy since she'd come to the ranch. "This is usual for me. Not for you."

She took the towel and pressed the white terry cloth to her face. She'd sit up just as soon as she had the energy. "My sister quit her job." She winced behind the towel, wishing she'd kept her mouth shut. But she supposed it was better than blurting out Nikki's *other* news.

"She works at the same place you did, doesn't she?"

"Huffington." Belle dropped her arms, the towel clutched in one hand. Cage was standing near the foot of the bench. "She was the boss's right hand, in fact."

"Afraid that means you're not going to be welcomed back to the clinic with open arms when your... leave...is over?"

Forget aching, tired muscles. She popped off the bench. "No. The thought hadn't even occurred to me," she snapped. "Not that I expect you to believe that I—a *Day*— could be concerned about something outside of myself." She brushed past him, hating the way her voice shook. But his arm shot out, his hand wrapping around her arm.

"I'm sorry."

She shivered. Wanting badly to blame it on the night air drifting over her sweaty body. Knowing it was just as much because of the gruff tone in his voice and the way his knuckles were pressing against the side of her breast.

She tugged away from his hold, that wasn't really a hold at all when he let go of her so easily and she was grateful she hadn't betrayed the way he made her feel.

Without looking at him, she walked over to the sound system. Flipped the power, cutting off Paul McCartney midnote.

"I'm sorry, too," she whispered.

About so many things.

She walked out, leaving Cage standing there in the barn, surrounded by weights and mats and bars and balls, all procured with the intention of helping Lucy walk and run and dance again.

Just then, however, it felt to Belle as if she and Cage were the ones in need of walking lessons.

Chapter Ten

"What are they doing in there? I've only been gone ten minutes."

Belle looked up at Cage and shot out her arm, barring him from barreling into the barn. "They're dancing," she said, taking an extra step to keep her balance. She didn't have to keep her voice lowered. There was no possible way the kids inside the barn would hear a word they said outside the barn. The music was too loud.

"I don't *want* them dancing."

A sputter of laughter escaped before she could prevent it. "Don't be such a grouch." Belle wrapped her hands around his forearm, digging in her heels. "You agreed to this," she reminded.

The lights from inside the barn were dim, but the moon was full and bright. Easily clear enough to see his expression as he looked from her hands to his arm. Belle hastily released him and circled her fingers against her palms. For days now, she'd managed to keep her thoughts right where they belonged.

At least she had while she'd been awake.

Sleep? That was a whole other kettle of tuna.

"Just peek in then," she allowed. "See for yourself."

He angled his head so he could see through the open barn door without drawing attention to himself.

Belle chewed the inside of her lip, waiting. She knew what he'd see.

And she knew the moment he *did* see, for his hand suddenly flattened against the weathered red wood and he exhaled slowly.

His newly turned teenage daughter was dancing with a boy. Crutches and all.

"That's Drew Taggart's boy."

She swallowed, an image of Cage's face so close to hers flashing through her mind. "Yes."

"He's got his arms around her."

"Well," Belle smiled gently, "in a manner of speaking, he does." The truth was, Evan Taggart looked as if he was half-afraid to touch Lucy and Lucy looked as if she was equally unsure of the entire process. But they were surrounded by fifteen other couples in exactly the same situation and nobody was making a move to change it. "She was afraid everyone would dance except her." She leaned her shoulder against the wall, watching. "I think they're doing pretty well considering she's still using her crutches."

Cage shifted, moving behind her. A shiver danced down her spine that she couldn't hope to blame on anything other than him. He propped his hand above her head and leaned closer, obviously trying to follow Lucy and Evan's lurching progress around the balloon-bedecked interior.

She felt surrounded by him.

And because it wasn't entirely unpleasant—well, not at all unpleasant if she was honest with herself—she focused harder on the kids. She'd agreed to help chaperone this shindig. She couldn't very well do that when she was preoccupied by the wall of warm, male chest heating her back.

She felt parched but her trusty water bottle was empty, and she was afraid if she stuck her head in amongst the dancers to get another drink, the boys and girls would retreat again to their opposite corners the way they'd been for the first hour.

"Thirteen," Cage murmured. "I guess I blinked."

"They do grow up fast. Every time I turn around my nieces and nephews have grown a foot." She glanced up at him, only to find his focus not on his daughter, but on her. She forgot about being amused right along with the art of breathing.

For days she'd worked so hard at forgetting…things. And now, all that hard work was for naught. "Arnold," she blurted.

His gaze didn't seem to stray from her lips. "What?"

"Your name." A naughty breeze skipped over them, splaying her hair across her cheek.

He caught the strands, brushing them back. "I told you. It's unique."

Arnold wasn't the current rage, but it wasn't unique. She cast her mind about, but coherence was annoyingly elusive. "How long is it?" Why did he still have a lock of her hair between his fingers?

His eyebrows rose. "Excuse me?"

She turned, facing him. Putting some necessary space between them. Shoving her hair behind her shoulders. "Letters. Syllables."

"Six. Two."

Easily as tall as some of her stepbrothers. Tall enough that she could wear heels and press her lips against the curve of his brown, corded throat.

Her face went hot and she hoped to heaven that the moonlight wasn't bright enough to reveal that. "Six letters," she murmured. "Two syllables." Though she'd bet his height *was* right around six-two.

"You're shivering."

"No, I'm not." She quickly turned back around, looking inside the barn. The music had changed. Most of the couples still danced. Not Evan and Lucy. But the boy was handing Lucy a cup of soda, his expression verging on adoring.

"You are." Cage's hand cupped her shoulder.

Belle closed her eyes for a moment. "It's the breeze," she lied.

He didn't reply. But he lowered his hand. And she heard the scrape of his boots on the gravel and turned to see him walking toward the house.

She blinked. Well. Okay. So her imagination was running riot again.

She turned back to watch the goings-on inside the barn. As Murphy's Law often proved, just when the boys and girls were starting to really have fun, it would be nearly time for them to leave. The boys, at least. The girls were staying for an overnight.

She tilted her watch to the light. Less than an hour and the rides would start arriving. Even with carpooling, there were several cars needed. Given the surprising occurrence of a party being held on the Lazy-B, the adults who'd brought their sons and daughters had admirably contained their curiosity. But she'd bet her paycheck that once they were back in town, the phone lines started buzzing.

"Here."

She nearly jumped out of her skin. Cage had returned. And he was tossing a plaid wool jacket over her shoulders.

Gads. It smelled like new-mown hay and fresh air with a dollop of coffee. It smelled like *him*. She clutched the collar with both hands, keeping it from sliding off her shoulders. "Thanks." The thing did nothing for her shivers, however. And the faint twist of his lips implied that he knew it.

Particularly when he scooped her hair free of the jacket and let it drift over her shoulders. "You don't wear your hair loose very often."

She hurriedly turned back to watch the youths. "No." It came out more of a croak, and she felt her face heat. "It gets in the way." That was better. A little less amphibian.

"Why not cut it?"

She shrugged. The slick lining of the jacket slid over her bare shoulders. Proving that she really was losing her mind. It was an ageless woolen jacket with a crinkling, polyester lining, for God's sake. Not seductive lingerie. "Lazy, I guess." She shoved her arms through the sleeves. The cuffs hung well below her fingertips. She probably looked like a clown. Hardly seductive.

Which she wasn't aiming for anyway. Right?

"You, lazy? That what gets you outta bed to jog around this place nearly every morning?"

How could the man be aware of things occurring when he was out doing the rancher thing? She marshaled her thoughts with some difficulty. "Easier to pull it back in a ponytail than mess with some shorter style. And the weight keeps the waves more or less controllable."

"Ever had it cut?"

"Of course." She had it trimmed regularly. "Never more than an inch or two, though. Cage—" She turned to face him, only to find whatever she'd planned to say flying right out of her head.

He'd sifted his fingers through the long ends of her hair. "Whose shirt was it?"

"Hmm?"

"The shirt you put on that weekend I came to your house." His fingers trailed along her jaw. Came perilously close to her lips.

Her mind was five steps behind the times. "Umm, I don't—"

"Hell with it," he murmured. His hand slid behind her head, cupping her nape, tilting her head back.

Belle froze, disbelief warring with anticipation. She wasn't sure which would win out, but it didn't matter, because Cage lowered his head and pressed his lips against hers and her senses simply exploded.

Her hands were pressed against his chest. She could feel his heavy heartbeat. She knew there were good reasons she should be pushing him away. Knew it.

She just couldn't manage to put her finger on one of those reasons right at the moment.

And then she stopped worrying about it altogether as the taste of him overwhelmed everything else.

Somehow, his arms had circled her, beneath the jacket. Her thin shirt was no barrier against his fingertips, which strolled up and down her spine. She shivered again.

"You're not cold." She felt his murmur against her lips.

"No."

The moment she answered, he took advantage, his tongue finding hers. Her knees dissolved. Had she ever felt a kiss down to her toes? Beyond? She arched against him, arms snaking around his shoulders, fingers seeking the shape of his head. Her muscles liquefied even while white-hot energy blasted through her.

Her head fell back as his mouth dragged over her jaw. Found her neck. Overhead, the stars whirled. Pounding music throbbed in the air, vibrating through their bodies.

This was not effective chaperoning, she thought hazily. "Cage—"

His mouth covered hers again, swallowing her half-hearted stab at sensibility. And when he finally did lift his head, she gave a soft moan of protest.

He made a rough sound and pressed her head to his shoulder. "This is a bad idea."

She nodded. Her fingers were knotted in his chambray shirt as surely as his fingers were tangled in her hair.

He muttered an oath. Tipped her head back. She didn't know what to say. Then he swore softly again. Pressed a hard kiss to her lips, before deliberately stepping away.

She swayed a little.

"I don't have time for this." His voice was quiet. Rough.

And even though his expression was as ragged as his voice, the words stung. "You kissed *me*," she reminded. "I wasn't chasing after you."

His gaze angled her way. "Did I say you were?"

"You—" No. He hadn't said that. But she'd been accused of chasing after Scott—which she hadn't been—but the humiliating memory of it lived on. And there was still the tacit warning he'd given her when he'd told her why Lucy's last therapist had been sent on her way.

"No." She raked back her hair, dismayed to see her hands were shaking.

Giggles gave them a very slim warning before a gaggle of girls darted out of the barn. They nearly skidded to a halt as they spied Belle and Cage. "Oh, good." Anya Johannson was the tallest of the three. "Lucy wants to cut her cake now. Is that okay?"

Belle couldn't prevent her quick glance at Cage. "Sure." She found a smile from somewhere and pinned it on her face, answering when he seemed to have no inclination to do so. "Good idea, actually," she went on, glancing at her watch as she followed the girls inside. "The boys will be leaving soon." And come morning, as soon as she could, she'd be leaving, as well, for the weekend.

She had a date to buttonhole her sister for some answers. She'd talked to Nikki on the phone twice since her sister had dropped the news. Nikki had been frustratingly closemouthed. She'd even warned Belle not to come see her.

Fat chance.

Cage followed her into the barn. He lit the candles on the cake and the kids sang. Lucy blew. Belle cut. Kids ate. The barn was filled with chatter and laughter. The time passed quickly enough, before the first headlights bounced over the ground outside the barn announcing the arrival of the first ride. But it seemed to Belle that the minutes crept because every ticking moment of them she was excruciatingly conscious of Cage's presence.

He didn't have time for "this." Did he honestly think that *she* did?

After what seemed an eternity, he disappeared along with the last of the departing boys, leaving Belle to deal with getting the girls settled. No small task. But she finally got the girls staying behind bedded down snug as bugs in Lucy's bedroom. They easily covered every spare inch of floor and bed space. When she finally closed the door on their whispers and giggles, she was vaguely surprised that some of them hadn't decided to bunk in the shower.

She was in the kitchen, trying to restore some order when Cage reappeared. She ignored him and continued tying up the trash bag that bulged with discarded plates and cups. She started to take it outside, but he silently took the bag from her and went out himself. When he came back, her hands were buried in soapy bubbles, the sleeves of the jacket rolled up to her elbows.

"When I asked you to stick around for the party I didn't mean you had to pull maid duty."

"When it comes to my pitching in around here you've made your feelings abundantly clear." She rinsed a pretty glass bowl that was probably older than she was and carefully set it down on the towel she'd spread on the counter.

"Yet you continue doing whatever you want." He scooped up the last few pretzels in a bowl before she could dump them out and plunge the bowl into the hot, soapy water.

"Yes, well, maybe I think you have enough to deal with without having to wash a few dishes."

"I don't need anyone's pity."

"Fortunately you don't have it." Her voice was stiff. "Nobody would be so stupid as to offer it, believe me. So why don't you go sit out on the porch again. Do whatever it is that you do when most normal people are sleeping."

He crunched through the pretzels. Deliberately set her aside then picked up the stack of remaining dishes and shoved them in the sink, splashing suds over his arms and chest.

He looked so much like a boy having a tantrum that she couldn't help the bubble of laughter that rose most inappropriately in her.

He glared at her.

She bit her lip, composing herself, and picked up a clean dish towel. Began drying the dishes. After a moment, she heard him sigh. "Lucy looked like she was having a great time." His voice wasn't quite grudging.

"Yes." She opened an overhead cupboard and began stacking the dishes inside. But when she would have dragged over a chair to reach the highest shelf, Cage took the glassware from her and did it himself.

It was positively domestic.

Utterly surreal.

"How long were you and Lucy's mother married?" She nearly chewed off her tongue, cursing her lack of discretion.

He pulled the stopper in the sink and watched the bubbles gurgle down the drain. "Why?" His voice was tight.

"Curiosity," she admitted huskily. She knew what the man tasted like now and her curiosity could no longer be contained.

He was silent for a long moment. Then seemed to shrug off his reticence. "We were together, more or less—usually less—for about seven months. She never lived here at the ranch."

Belle frowned. So little time. She wanted more details, but she'd already asked questions she shouldn't have. "You were really young," she observed instead.

"Old enough to get a marriage license. Sandi was nearly twenty-one."

Older than he was, then. She tried to picture him as a teenage groom. Had he been reluctant? Insistent? Blinded by love for the woman who was carrying his child—a child who would be living, breathing family for a boy who'd lost so much?

She folded the towel he'd discarded into neat thirds. Then thirds again. "You don't sound as if you're still nursing a broken heart. That's what some people say, you know. To explain why you don't date anyone from town."

He snorted softly. "Some people. Suppose you believe everything you read, too."

She shook her head, all too aware that he hadn't actually denied it. "How'd you meet?"

He turned around, crossing his arms over his chest,

an action that only made him seem even broader. The man was both mother and father to his child, and she'd never met anyone more masculine.

She quickly unfolded the towel. It would never dry with those tight folds. He was watching her, and she hastily draped it over the oven handle.

"Want to make sure there's no hidden wife in the wings when we end up in bed together?"

She went still, emotions bolting through her. Foolish of her to assume that *her* personal business had remained personal. After all, if Brenda Wyatt knew about the debacle with Scott Langtree, then she'd have undoubtedly informed the rest of the Weaver population. Which apparently included even a reclusive rancher who was, himself, the brunt of considerable conjecture.

"I guess you've listened to your own share of gossip. And, just for the record, you and I are *not* going to end up in bed together."

He lifted an eyebrow, his gaze dropping to her lips.

She flushed, heat streaking through her with the tenacity of a forest fire. "I don't sleep with men I don't love." She didn't care if she sounded prissy or not. She was old enough to know what she did and did not want. Wasn't she? And meaningless sex was not something she'd ever wanted to indulge in.

Only it wouldn't be meaningless, would it?

"Did you love him, then? The guy of the white shirt? Keep it as a memento before you decided he was a snake?"

"You're really preoccupied with that shirt," she murmured, trying to banish the whispering thought of meaningless versus meaningful. "If you must know, I think my stepbrother Tristan left it behind a long time ago when he and Hope were dating. It's her house, you know."

"There's not much else that's sexier than a woman wearing a man's shirt and little else. But no man wants to see a woman *he* wants wearing another man's shirt."

Well, that was blunt. The man went for days, *weeks,* without hardly saying a word, and in one evening he'd kissed her silly *and* admitted to wanting her.

She snatched up a bottle of water. Fiddled with the cap. Put the bottle back on the table for fear she'd just spill it over herself.

"Must be inconvenient to want something you despise," she murmured. And wished like fury that she didn't want, so badly, for him to deny it. She wasn't supposed to care how he felt about her. She was only supposed to get Lucy back on track, and maybe, just maybe regain some of her professional confidence in the process.

That's not all you want.

She ignored the little voice.

Cage still hadn't responded and she felt something foolish inside her wilt.

Exactly what she deserved for getting too involved with her patients.

Cage isn't your patient.

A muffled shriek of laughter startled her. The girls, of course.

She brushed her hands down her thighs. "Well. Good night, Cage. Try to get some sleep for once."

He remained silent. Big surprise.

But she felt his gaze on her as she left the kitchen and padded up the stairs.

It wasn't until she closed herself in the relative safety and solitude of the bedroom next to Cage's that she realized she was still wearing his jacket.

She lifted the worn wool close to her nose and closed her eyes, inhaling the faint scent of him while impossible images danced in her mind.

The truth was, it would be a miracle if any of them slept at all that night.

Chapter Eleven

"Got a problem?"

Belle pressed her forehead to the steering wheel for a moment. She'd gotten up early, knowing Lucy and her pals would still be sleeping, and hoping Cage would have been doing the same.

Foolish of her to think that of a man who never seemed to sleep.

She looked sideways at him through the opened window and dropped her hand away from the key. She'd been trying—and failing—to get the Jeep started. The engine kept dying. "What gave it away?"

The corner of his lip lifted and her stomach gave a funny little dip. She quickly looked down, but the sight of his long fingers absently brushing through Strudel's ruff was no less disturbing.

"Pop the hood." He gestured toward the front of her

vehicle and the unbuttoned denim shirt he wore rippled, baring a slice of chest. "I'll take a look," he prompted when she just sat there like a ninny. The sideways look he cast her had her stomach dancing again. "Unless you've got a wrench handy somewhere and plan to attack the engine yourself with it?"

"So funny." She flexed her fingers, blocking out the insistent and too fresh memory from the night before, and pulled the lever to release the truck's hood.

She'd feel better—about everything—once she saw her sister. She drummed her fingers on the steering wheel for a moment, then climbed out and went around to stand by him. She braced herself for Strudel's loving assault, but Cage said a quiet word that had the dog settling on his haunches.

She looked under the hood, managing not to skitter away when he shifted, closing the distance between them. But he merely reached into the engine.

She watched him fiddle with this, tinker with that.

She could have been staring into noodle soup for all the sense it made to her.

Then he straightened. His fingers were covered with black smudges. "Try it again."

She blindly climbed behind the wheel once more. Automatically turned the key as she'd done a million times before. Thank goodness for habits because the sight of his chest, up close, was still occupying her retinas.

The engine started, spat a little then settled in with a purr.

"How does he do that?" she asked no one in particular. "Thanks," she said loudly.

He shut the hood and brushed his hands together, watching her through the windshield. "You should get it into the mechanic soon," he warned. Then the corners of his lips quirked up a little.

For a moment she simply forgot how to breathe.

Then he waved and headed back to the house. Strudel bounded after him.

Belle sank into her seat, her breath coming out of her with a little *whoosh*. She was actually trembling.

Her purse suddenly chirped and she nearly jumped out of her skin. She grabbed the thing from the passenger seat where she'd dumped it, and dug inside for the ringing cell phone. She barely had the presence of mind to look at the displayed number.

It was her mother.

Belle swallowed and quickly pushed the phone back into the depths of the purse where it continued squawking.

Guilt congealing in her stomach, she eyed the purse, then quickly shoved it behind the seat and turned up the volume on the radio until she could no longer hear the summons.

Giving the brick house another last look, she pulled the Jeep around and drove away. The sooner she got to Cheyenne to see her sister, the better.

A nice plan.

She still believed it had a chance of working, too, even when—two hours later—she was at her little house in Weaver, trying to figure out how to borrow a car because her Jeep was still sitting on the side of the highway where it had given out.

Handy that one of her stepbrothers was the sheriff.

Sawyer had driven her the rest of the way to town and assured her that he'd have the Jeep towed in for repairs. Even more fortunate that he'd received a call and hadn't had time to stick around and chat when he'd dropped her off at her place.

It had been easy to love her stepfamily. They'd all welcomed her and Nikki with open hearts when Gloria married Squire. But she wasn't ignorant of their ways, particularly the men.

Steamrollers, all of them.

But none of them had anything on Gloria. She'd wrapped them all, to a one, around her finger without so much as turning a hair. And even though there were plenty of Clays around who would lend Belle a vehicle so she could drive to Cheyenne, there was no way she could count on that information not getting back to Gloria. And given the fact that Belle hadn't been back to Cheyenne in months, she knew her mother would be suspicious about Belle's urgency in getting there, now.

Weaver didn't possess anything so convenient as a car-rental agency, either.

She tried calling Nikki, hoping she could convince her sister to drive *to* Weaver, but her sister wasn't answering *her* phone, either. Probably hiding out from it, much the same way Belle was.

Hoping she wasn't creating a bigger mess, she quickly dialed the Lazy-B. And much later that afternoon, Belle sat alongside Cage as they drove to Cheyenne.

Too bad Lucy had fallen asleep. She'd chattered nonstop for a solid hour before succumbing to the aftereffects of her birthday party. And Belle could only stare out the window at the scenery whizzing past for so long when it did nothing to keep her thoughts safely occupied.

She glanced back at Lucy, sprawled on the rear seat of Cage's SUV. Deliberately waking the girl so she'd start gibber jabbering again would be selfish.

She faced forward. "Thanks again," she murmured. "For letting me hitch along with you." Even though Cage had begun taking Lucy again on the visits to see his mother, she still felt presumptuous. And warily surprised that Cage had readily offered to drive to Weaver and pick her up before making their trip. It would be evening before they arrived. "I guess I really lucked out in catching you and Lucy before you left."

His sideways glance touched on her and it was like being physically dipped in something warm. Something intoxicating.

"We weren't planning to go this week," he said after a moment. "We'd barely started getting Lucy's friends rousted out of their sleeping bags when you called."

She stared. "Then…why?"

"Obviously you're anxious to get there. And Luce always likes visiting my mother at the care center."

She absorbed that. Kept waiting for some dark comment, some grimace, some *something* from him to remind her of the reasons his mother was in the care center in the first place.

But there was nothing at all conveying that in his expression.

There was nothing but a long, slow look from eyes that should have been too pale to have the singeing effect they did.

She swallowed, and trained her own gaze front and

center, straight out over the hood of the vehicle. "I see." But she didn't. Not really. "Well. Thank you."

"You're welcome." His tone was dry.

She looked back at Lucy. "*She's* not used to so little sleep at night."

"Wouldn't matter if she'd slept twelve hours." He smoothly passed a slow-moving semi. "For driving company, she's a bust." His lip quirked. "She passes out as soon as she hears the sound of the tires on the highway. Always has."

Oh, Lord. She was staring at the slashing little dimple that had appeared in his lean cheek. She blindly began fumbling in her purse. "Guess she finds it a soothing sound."

"Guess so. When she was a baby, I could get her to sleep sometimes by strapping her in her car seat and driving down to the gate. You mining for gold in there?"

She closed her hand over an object and pulled it out, relieved to see it was something useful. "Just these." She shook the little tin, making the mints inside rattle softly. "Want one?"

"Is that a hint?"

She flushed. The man tasted better than any mint. "No."

He chuckled softly and held out his palm.

She dropped a mint in it, and popped one in her own mouth then put the tin back in her purse. As a distraction it had been much too brief.

"Did you have to drive her around a lot?" She sounded a little frantic, and swallowed. "To get her to sleep, I mean," she added much more calmly.

"Enough."

Which only made her wonder more how he'd managed at such a young age. "You didn't have any help with her?"

"There was an insurance settlement," he said after a moment. "Eventually, anyway. It came through about the time Lucy was born. Got my mother settled in the care center. Hired a few hands for a while. High-school kids who needed to earn some extra cash."

"*You* were a high-school kid," she murmured.

"Honey, I was born old."

Honey. Nearly every male in the entire state called women that. It meant nothing.

It…meant…nothing. Any minute now, he'd start calling her *Miss Day* in that stubborn way he had.

"You're not old," she dismissed.

"Why? Because you're less than a handful of years younger than me?"

He was teasing her. She scrambled through the surprise of that. "I'm certainly not about to think I'm on the cusp of being old," she said lightly. "Besides. I think *old* is more a state of mind."

"Spoken with the blitheness of someone who hasn't had her child look at her with rolling eyes."

Belle smiled and glanced back at Lucy. Sound, still. "She *is* pretty great."

"Despite me," he murmured.

She flushed again remembering her statement—a serious statement—to that very effect. She turned a little in the seat, facing him. "I still don't understand why you wouldn't let her go on that field trip, Cage." Her voice was low. "If it was a matter of cost—"

"It wasn't." His voice had gone flat as the look he gave her.

She nodded, even though she didn't necessarily believe him.

"I didn't want her in Chicago."

She tugged at her ear. "What are you going to do the next time a field trip comes up? Each class tries to take a cultural trip each year. They're often out of state."

"As long as it's not Chicago."

"Because of her grandparents, or because it's where that private school she's interested in is located?" She straightened in her seat again, certain he wouldn't respond to that.

"Take your pick," he said in a low voice. "I'm not going to lose my daughter to either one."

Her lips parted, but no words came for a long moment. "You could never lose Lucy, Cage. She loves you too much."

But his lips twisted and he said no more.

The sun was setting by the time they hit the outskirts of Cheyenne. Belle pointed out the directions to Nikki's place.

He stopped at the curb in front of the town house. "Looks dark."

Truer words. There wasn't a single light burning from the windows of Nikki's home. Even the porch was stone-cold black.

Lucy, awake since they'd hit town, hung her head over the seat. "Was she expecting you?"

"She knew I was coming. She's probably just out getting a bite for dinner." Belle smiled with more certainty than she felt. "Don't worry. I have a key." She grabbed up her purse and pushed open the door with more haste than was dignified. There was nothing about the trip that hadn't been disturbing. Not sitting along-side Cage. Not listening to the things he'd said. Not speculating about the things he hadn't. She slid off the high seat. "Thanks again for the lift."

"Wait."

She halted long enough to see Cage scribbling on the back of a small piece of paper he pulled from the console.

"Here." He held out the note. "That's where we stay when we're in town and my cell-phone number. Call."

It was more an order than a request and her spine stiffened. "I appreciate the ride, but really, Nikki's car is in *much* better shape than mine. I'll be back at the Lazy-B on Monday as usual."

"Oh, please, Belle. Drive back with us tomorrow. She could even come with us to have supper, right, Dad?" Lucy smiled hopefully.

Despite Cage's knowing expression, Belle couldn't make herself disappoint the girl entirely. She plucked the note from his fingers. "It's really not necessary," she assured. And probably not wise. Being cooped up again in such close quarters. And Lucy wouldn't be much of a chaperone, given Cage's warning that the girl hit the *z's* on any road trip.

"Then we'll wait with you."

"Excuse me?"

Cage's face was set. "You heard me." He turned off the engine.

She made a soft sound, not sure whether she was charmed or exasperated. "It's not as if you're dropping me on some dangerous street corner. This is my sister's home in a perfectly respectable neighborhood."

"Humor me."

She tossed up her hands. "Fine. Whatever. I'll *call*."

"Good." He started the vehicle once more. "We'll wait until you get inside."

Obviously, arguing would be pointless, so she headed up the geranium-lined walk, digging through her purse again. Fortunately, Nikki's house key *was* still on Belle's key chain, and she fumbled only a little in the dark before pushing open the door and stepping inside. She flipped on the porch light and waved at the idling vehicle.

He didn't drive away until she'd closed the door.

Belle leaned back against it, listening to the soft rumble of the departing truck. Then she flipped another switch and warm light pooled through the entry from the two buffet lamps Nikki had situated on a narrow foyer table. Even though she knew her sister wasn't there, she still walked through the place, upstairs and down, calling her sister's name.

There was a folded note on the kitchen table with Belle's name written on it. She dumped her purse and Cage's note on the table, picked up Nikki's and read.

"If you're here, then you didn't listen, and I love you anyway. I'm okay, but I'm not ready to talk about any of this yet. I'll see you at Angel's birthday party. Love, Nik."

"Well, fudgebuckets." She dropped the note and it fluttered to the tabletop, rustling the scrap of paper that Cage had insisted she take. The hotel name and phone number were written in bold, slashing strokes.

No nonsense. That was Cage Buchanan.

She wandered back into the living room and threw

herself down on her sister's squishy couch. That day's newspaper was sitting on the coffee table. Proof that Nikki hadn't been hiding out for too long.

She sat forward and pulled the paper closer. Flipped it open to the classified section and ran her eye down the rental listings.

Several in the right area of town, conveniently located nearby the clinic. Decent rent. Good space.

She flipped the paper over, folding it in half.

Perfectly decent rentals and not a one of them held any appeal.

Or maybe it was the fact that moving back to Cheyenne—as she'd always planned to do—was no longer as appealing as it had once been. Because every time she contemplated it, her mind got stuck over a sturdy little brick house and the bronze-haired man who lived there.

"Oh, Nikki," she murmured. "What kind of messes are we getting ourselves into?"

She went back into the kitchen to use the phone there, and dialed the number Cage had left. She nearly lost her nerve as it rang. But on the third, he answered.

"Hi," she greeted. "You guys still up for some supper?" *Say no. Say yes. Better yet, just shoot me now and put me out of this insane misery.*

"Find your sister?"

She crossed her fingers childishly. "Yes. Well, no, just a little crossing of our wires. So…have you fed Lucy, yet?" She could hear the girl in the background, asking Cage if it was Belle on the line.

"In the thirty minutes since we dropped you off?" He sounded amused.

Only thirty minutes? It seemed longer. She tucked a loose strand of hair behind her ear. "I'll take that as a no. If you, um, want to come back here, I can throw something together."

"No." His answer came a little too fast and some of her nervousness dissolved in favor of humor. She cooked regularly for Lucy, but she knew there wasn't much of anything that she'd left that Cage had tried. He'd labeled her cooking as inedible from the get-go and hadn't changed his opinion since. "I mean, Lucy's begging for pizza. I imagine if you flash those Bambi-brown eyes of yours at the cook, he'll make you some wheat-vegetarian thing."

Bambi eyes? She glanced in the window-fronted cabinet above the counter. And shook herself when she realized what she was doing. "All right, but I'm paying. Hey—" she was prepared for his immediate protest, and spoke over it. "It's the least I can do, given the chauffeur job you took on."

"Then breakfast is on me before the return trip," he said after a moment.

Her imagination went riot. Oatmeal and raisins, she thought desperately, trying to counter it. A useless endeavor, it seemed, since her imagination was most definitely in the driver's seat.

"Belle?"

"What?"

"I said we'd be there in twenty minutes." His voice was dry and she had a terrifying suspicion that he was perfectly aware of the reason for her distraction.

"Right," she said briskly. "I'll be ready."

She hung up and sat there in the kitchen. Then, realizing how time was ticking, she darted upstairs. Nikki had been moaning over Belle's lack of interest in fashion for years. If her sister weren't so stubborn, she'd undoubtedly have enjoyed the sight of Belle rummaging through her closet.

With a bare five minutes to spare, she stood in front of Nikki's mirror. Cowardice accosted her. She rarely wore dresses and she'd never filled out one the way her sister did. But before she could change back into her jeans and T-shirt, the doorbell rang.

Her nervous system went into hyperdrive. She looked longingly at her jeans.

The doorbell rang again.

She could almost hear Nikki's musical laughter in her head.

"I'm ready," she called out, clattering in the unfamiliar heels down the steps, the skirt of the floaty sundress flying around her ankles.

She skidded to a stop on the tile at the door and blew out a deep breath. She'd be composed if it killed her.

Then she opened the door and silently blessed Nikki and her well-endowed closet when Cage's eyes sharpened, taking her in from head to toe, a look so encompassing that it made her skin feel too snug.

It was *not* a bad feeling. At all.

"I'm ready," she said again.

She just wasn't quite ready to admit to herself what she was ready for.

Chapter Twelve

"So. You do eat junk food." Cage watched Belle across the red-and-white checked tablecloth. The jar in the center of the table glowed from the lit candle inside it. The place was redolent with the smell of sausages, onions and garlic.

Nirvana.

And there Belle sat, looking like some fairy-tale fantasy with her long, waving hair providing the dark cloak around that surprising dress. Innocence and seduction all rolled into one intoxicating woman who was eating her wedge of pizza—the real kind, not some bastardized "healthy" version of it—backward. From the crust to the tip. Licking cheese from her fingertips. Gustily working her way through a healthy helping of pepperoni, black olive and mushroom.

She'd raised her eyebrows at his comment, a

mischievous dimple flirting from her smooth cheek. "Call the health-food police," she challenged.

Lucy's elbows were propped on the table, her chin on her hands. "Belle's cooking is good, too, Dad," she said loyally.

"That's all right, Lucy," Belle assured her easily. "Your dad doesn't have to try my cooking. Some people are afraid of—"

"Eating birdseed?"

"—trying something new," she finished, her eyes laughing.

"I'd sooner eat Rory's oats."

Belle smiled, obviously not offended. "Might be good for you," she suggested blandly, and lifted the remains of her pizza slice.

He watched her work her way toward the tip. Given the presence of his daughter, he tried to pretend that Belle's obvious relish of her food was not turning him on. "Why start with the crust?"

She glanced from the remaining wedge, little more than a glob of gooey cheese on her fingertips, to him. "Saving the best for last," she said, as if it ought to have been obvious.

His mind, and his damn body, took a left turn at that, right down horny lane. What other kind of "bests" would Belle savor right up to the end?

He grabbed his iced tea and chugged the remaining half glass.

Belle was eyeing his plate where an untouched slice still sat. "You weren't very hungry?"

There was hunger and there was hunger. And he was damn near starved. "Guess not."

"Whenever I take more than I can eat, Dad tells me my eyes were bigger than my stomach."

"Well, right now, your eyes look in danger of falling asleep." Belle finished off her pizza slice, her own lashes drooping. But it wasn't tiredness on her face.

It was an expression of utter bliss.

Cage pushed back from the table. "I'll be back." He ignored the surprised looks—in duplicate—they gave him and headed toward the front of the crowded, cozy pizza joint, maneuvering his way through the line of people waiting for a table, and escaped out the front door.

He hauled in a long breath of cool, evening air, willing his body back under control. If he'd been a drinking man, he'd have found the nearest bottle of single malt and admired the curves of that.

But he didn't drink. There'd already been one Buchanan who'd done more than enough of that. And even though Cage knew his dad's habit hadn't contributed to his death, there'd been plenty of times it had contributed to Cage taking over the reins of the Lazy-B while his dad *was* alive.

He moved out of the way for a family to get to the door and walked along the sidewalk bordering the restaurant. Through one of the windows, he could see Lucy and Belle at the table, dark head and light, angled together companionably. The waiter stopped by the table and Belle smiled up at the kid.

Jesus.

He let out a harsh breath, walking farther, around the corner of the building and away from that winsome sight only to stop short.

Everything hot inside him froze, stone-cold at the sight of the woman standing there, eyeing him with considerably less shock than he felt.

Thirteen years—minus about six days—had passed since he'd laid eyes on Sandi Oldham. Then, her hair had been a wild mane around her shoulders, her cheeks smudged with running mascara. Not because she'd just handed over their baby to him for good, but because her credit-card limit had been reached and she wasn't able to buy the plane ticket to get her to Brazil where there was some dance troupe she wanted to get hooked up with.

Now, her gold hair was pulled back in a sophisticated-looking twist at the back of her head, and her face was cruelly perfect.

"What'd you do," he asked after a moment. "Hire someone to follow us?"

Her eyes flickered, and he knew he was right.

He also knew he had a piece of legalese that said she had no right to be around the child she'd borne but had never mothered. He turned on his heel, but she jogged on treacherous heels until she stood in his path.

"Wait."

"Get out of my way, Sandi. You have something to say, say it through your parents' lawyers. God knows, they have enough of 'em." He kept moving.

She shifted, walking backward, still trying to block his way. "Cage, wait—"

"No." He had to remind himself that—whatever his personal feelings were for her—she was equally responsible for the existence of Lucy. Wishing her back to the far corners of the earth had to suffice.

He brushed past her. She smelled as expensive as she'd ever smelled. Only he wasn't a seventeen-year-old kid still reeling from his parents' accident, and that expensive scent that once had him salivating only made his head ache now.

Give him rainwater fresh.

"Cage." Her voice followed him. "I'm sorry. I didn't want it to be like this."

He frowned. Turned on her, incredulous. "Just how the hell did you think it *could* be?"

She approached, her skinny boots clicking like gunshots on the cracked sidewalk. "You surprised me, coming out of the restaurant like that. I just want to see her, Cage. She's my daughter, too."

"And she wouldn't even exist if I hadn't dragged you, kicking and screaming out of that doctor's office before he performed the abortion." He remembered the day clearly. More missed school, in too many days of them after the accident, when he'd had to fight everyone to keep hold of what was left of his life—the ranch. Finishing high school had seemed the least of his worries when there'd been people intent on putting him in foster care somewhere. As if he hadn't already had a man's responsibilities on the Lazy-B. He'd hated people getting in his business ever since.

So he mostly avoided people when he could.

"I was young. Scared," Sandi said. She moistened her lips, looking vulnerable.

He wasn't fooled. There'd been nothing vulnerable about Sandi. Not from the get-go. And, in physical years at least, he'd been younger than she.

He knew in his bones that she hadn't changed her

spots in the years since. He'd be damned if he'd lose his daughter to her after all this time, but even more, he'd damn Sandi to hell for all eternity if she hurt Lucy.

He'd already cursed her parents there and back again for that horse.

"I don't give a f—," he reined in his anger. "You signed away your parental rights a long time ago," he reminded her flatly. Right along with signing the divorce decree. He may have been still a kid, and he may have done some stupid damn things along the way, but he hadn't been a complete fool.

She didn't try to deny it, at least. "I know she's inside with that woman you hired." Sandi looked toward the restaurant door. "Belle Day. Nice work, that, Cage. I must admit, I was surprised to hear that name in connection with you."

His fingers curled into fists since he couldn't very well wrap them around her neck where they ached to go. He was glad the windows near the corner didn't afford a view of the table where Belle and Lucy still sat. "Don't go there, Sandi," he warned softly. If she thought she'd already won, she was sadly mistaken.

She angled a look his way. A look that may have acquired some subtlety over the years, but was still purely calculating. "You should have taken me seriously months ago, Cage. All I wanted was to have a relationship with my daughter. But no. You had to have her all to yourself. And now," she shook her head, looking regretful. "You're paying the price. Because now, you have to deal with my parents."

There was nothing but truth in her words and they still sounded vile. Then she reached out and touched the collar of his shirt, her fingertips slowly moving down the buttons. Her head tilted back and she looked up at him. "We can still work something out, Cage. You have to know that I've been desperate. Otherwise I'd never have brought my parents into this. I told you long ago what they were like. Always controlling everything with their money. I don't want Lucy subjected to them, either, but if it's the only way I can see her, then—"

He wrapped his hand around her wrist, trapping her fingers. "What, exactly, are you suggesting?"

She leaned in another inch. "You're the only one I ever married, Cage."

He watched her about as closely as he'd watch a coiled snake. A snake could be taken care of with a well-aimed, sharp shovel blade, though.

"We were still kids and marriage was your price," he reminded. No matter the struggles his parents had faced before his family was destroyed, he believed in family. To the end of his days. Sandi had given him a family, but she'd never been part of it, herself.

"Maybe marrying you was one thing I did do right," she whispered. "You're looking good, Cage." With her free hand, she reached up and brushed her fingers through his hair. "As good as I always expected. And things weren't always bad between us. We had some good times."

He wondered how far she was willing to go in her little pretense. How he could use it to his advantage, turn it against her and get her the hell out of his—Lucy's— life.

"We were wondering what was keeping you."

Cold slithered down his spine at the cool tone and

he looked over Sandi's head to see Belle standing on the sidewalk watching them.

Her expression was calm, but he could see the tempest brewing in her dark eyes. "I'll be inside in a minute," he told her. Willed her to turn and go back. To be with Lucy, because there was no contest in his mind with whom his daughter would be safer.

Protected.

It sure wasn't the blonde who'd given Lucy her genes.

And wasn't this a helluva time to realize just how much he *did* trust Belle?

For a tense moment, Belle eyed him. Looked from him to Sandi. Then she turned, her pretty dress flaring around her delicate ankles, and headed back inside the restaurant.

Relief eased the vise inside him, though he was smart enough to know it was only temporary. He was also smart enough to know his relief was only partially for Lucy.

Belle consumed the rest of it.

As she'd been consuming him all along.

He released Sandi's hand and stepped back so she'd get her fingers out of his hair. "Go back to Europe. Or wherever you've been hanging your broom these last years. There's no way you're going to see Lucy." He'd put Sandi over his shoulder and lock her away somewhere and take his chances with the law over it, if it came to that.

"You're going to regret this, Cage. It'd be easier to deal with me than my parents."

He eyed her. Even though he'd known it in his head, it was still a relief to realize that—face-to-face with her—she left him cold.

"I'll take my chances," he said.

She stared at him for a long moment, lips tight with displeasure. Then she muttered an oath and turned toward the parking lot. He watched her climb in an expensive sports car and didn't go back in the restaurant until she'd driven away with a squeal of tires and a grinding clutch that was criminal in such a vehicle.

Inside, he paused among the throng still awaiting tables and consciously tamped down the anger burning inside him. He caught their waiter and paid the check, then headed over to the table where Lucy and Belle waited.

"Ready?"

Lucy nodded sleepily and reached for her crutches. Belle didn't look at him as she stood also and gathered up the foil-wrapped leftover slices. "I need to get the check from the waiter." Her voice was still cool.

"It's taken care of."

Her jaw tightened. "It was supposed to be my treat."

He tucked his hand around her elbow—absorbing the fine shimmer that went through them both at the contact—and nudged her after Lucy, who was carefully making her way through the crush of tables, chairs and bodies. "Next time."

She shot him a look. Startled. Maybe tempted despite what she thought she'd seen?

"There's going to be a next time?" Her voice wasn't cool now. It was soft. Wistful.

Just that easily, the frozen wasteland left behind by his ex-wife went molten. His thumb stroked over her inner arm. "What do you think?"

"I thought you didn't have *time* for this," she said,

barely loud enough for him to hear over the conversations swirling around them.

But the masses had parted for Lucy to make her way more easily to the door, and he didn't want his daughter going out there without him first.

Just in case.

He reluctantly slid his hand away from Belle's arm and slid in front of Lucy to push open the door. Fortunately, he was parked very near the door, and he had the women stowed inside within minutes. And there was no sign of the Porsche having returned.

"Dad?" Lucy was sprawling in the rear seat. "Can you take me to the hotel first before you drop off Belle?"

He looked back at her. "What's wrong?"

She lifted her shoulder. "Nothing. I'm just tired. And my leg is kinda hurting."

And he wouldn't be leaving her unattended in a hotel room for any length of time. Not tonight.

"It's fine," Belle said softly, brushing his leg with her fingertips. "Go to the hotel."

She pulled her hand back quickly, but the whispering contact had more than done its job. His skin was singing. He grabbed her hand again. Ignoring the way she started when he flattened her palm beneath his and pressed it back against leg.

The warmth seared through his jeans, spearing upward. He was prepared for that. He just wasn't necessarily prepared to feel that warmth head further north than his crotch. But it did, and it was heading up his chest where his heart beat an oddly heavy beat.

"If Nikki's not at her place yet, I'll just grab a cab

ride back from the hotel," Belle added. Her voice had gone husky again.

Lucy looked pale in the dim light penetrating the windows from the parking lot. He gave up the brief idea of simply driving back to Weaver that very night. He turned forward and started the truck.

Belle didn't move her hand away, not even when he needed both of his to reverse out of the parking spot.

He drove back to the hotel, watching every set of headlights that seemed to follow them.

Just because you're paranoid doesn't mean they're not out to get you.

But there didn't seem to be any car paying them particular attention. And there was no sign of Sandi's car, either. She'd obviously had them followed—a task that had to have begun in Weaver—so there was no point in pretending that the woman didn't already know where they were staying.

He gave up watching the other cars and concentrated instead on getting to the hotel.

It was so obvious that Lucy was in more pain than she let on when they got there, that Cage just handed Belle the crutches and lifted his daughter in his arms, carrying her up to their room.

Belle trailed behind them, hurrying ahead when he jerked his chin at the room to use the key and open the door. She didn't know what was going on—who the woman had been with her hands in Cage's hair outside of the restaurant—but she knew that whatever "it" was, it was important. It was as if the lines of a familiar painting had changed. Ever so slightly.

And now she didn't know what she was looking at exactly.

The hotel offered complete suites. Belle followed him through the living-room area into the bedroom where he deposited Lucy on the wide bed. She set the crutches within easy reach, then turned to give them some privacy.

But Lucy caught her hand, staying her. "I've got a charley horse," she whispered.

Judging by the suddenly tense look in the girl's eyes, this time it was no pretense. Belle sat on the bed and tugged off Lucy's tennis shoe, carefully letting her fingers work up the girl's calf until she could feel what was going on.

Cage sat down on the other side of the bed, his eyes on Belle as she gently kneaded the painful knot loose. It took a while. Every time it seemed to ease up, Lucy would move, and another muscle went into spasm. Belle's hands ached a little by the time they'd licked the thing for good.

She sat back, realizing the position she'd ended up in on the bed chasing Lucy's muscle spasms—on her knees, her sister's pretty white dress shoved inelegantly between her thighs—was hardly attractive. She slid off the bed, tugging self-consciously at the dress.

"Here. Can you manage?" Cage handed over Lucy's pajamas from the small case they'd brought along.

Lucy nodded. She was already half asleep, barely murmuring a good-night when Cage leaned down and kissed her forehead.

Belle was in the living area when Cage left the bedroom. He pulled the door closed, his gaze angled toward her.

She swallowed and moved across the room, looking blindly out the large window at the end of the room. It looked out over an oval swimming pool. The pool was lit and it glowed, pale, bluish-white.

Like Cage's eyes, almost.

"So." She turned, hugging her elbows. "Who was the woman at the restaurant?"

Chapter Thirteen

Belle waited, tensely, as her question hovered in the air. She hadn't even attempted to make the question casual. Had she tried, she'd have failed miserably, making this even more humiliating.

"Nobody who matters," Cage said after a moment.

She wanted to believe him. Wanted to hear that *she* mattered, which was so far out of the realm of their nonrelationship that it scared her. "She looked like she knew you well." The sophisticated-looking blonde had had her fingers in Cage's hair, for pity's sake. Looking as though she was staking her claim right there on the sidewalk outside a bustling, family pizzeria.

He shook his head. As slowly and surely as he stepped closer to her. "She doesn't know me at all. Not anymore."

Belle's heart hovered in her throat, making breathing rather a challenge. She stiffened her spine a little.

Brushed her hands down the dress that she'd managed to wrinkle, crushing it the way she had on Lucy's bed. What on earth had possessed her to borrow the outfit from Nikki, anyway? If that smooth blonde was the type of woman Cage preferred… "Well. It's none of my business, anyway."

"You look pretty in the dress," he said.

Was she so easy to read? "I don't need meaningless compliments," she said stiffly.

"You think I don't mean it?" He stepped closer. "Fact is, you look pretty no matter what you're wearing. Red. Gray. White robe. It's all good. Believe me."

Panic streaked through her. She couldn't afford to forget who they were. *Where* they were. "Dagwood," she blurted.

His eyebrow peaked. "Pardon?"

"Oh. That's seven letters." Her feet backed up a step, which only made her bump the large air-conditioning unit attached to the wall beneath the window. Silly of her to have forgotten her shoes in Lucy's bedroom. She'd kicked them off before climbing completely onto the mattress. Another few inches of height on her part would have helped counter the overwhelming, intoxicating size of him.

As if.

"I told you." He stepped closer. "It's unique."

"Please," she sniffed. "Dagwood isn't unique?"

He shook his head, a faint smile hovering around the corners of his lips.

Belle couldn't sidestep him, or move backward any farther. She put out her hand, flattening it against his chest. "What's going on here, Cage?"

"You need me to draw you a map?" He didn't push her hand away. Merely pressed his fingers to her wrist, then slid them along the length of her arm. Curved around her bicep and traveled back again, seriously causing her elbow fits as he seemed to find every ridge and bump, before traveling onward, returning to her wrist.

Shivers danced under her skin.

She needed no map to follow the direction he was headed. "But…why?"

That hint of a smile left his face. His jaw cocked to one side for a moment, then centered again. "Because what I said last night 'bout not having time for this was bull. And I'm tired of pretending."

She decided discretion was the better part of valor, and lowered her hand from his chest, only to tuck both hands behind her back. Out of his temptation. Out of her own. "Your daughter is in the next room."

He made a nearly soundless, wry grunt. "You think I don't know that?"

No. She shook her head. She didn't think Cage would ever forget his daughter. He was too devoted. It was a significant portion of his appeal.

"She's asleep," he assured her after a moment. "She'll stay asleep unless she has a nightmare." He lifted his hand and she watched it, helpless to move, as it neared her face. When his fingers threaded, oh so easily, so gently, through the waves at her temple and glided through it, her muscles turned to warm, running wax. She felt her head falling back a little, like a too heavy bloom on its stalk, still seeking the sunlight.

He'd stepped closer. She could see the little scar below his lip so clearly. Had he gotten it as a rambunctious little boy? A headstrong teenager? "Cage—"

"I love your hair," he murmured, lifting his other hand to her head, also, and effectively cutting off her ability to think even ridiculous thoughts.

He lifted handfuls of her hair, and let it sift down, watching her from beneath heavy lids. His head drooped an inch closer to hers. "I love that you don't wear it loose very often. Then it's like this—" his jaw canted, then centered again and his hands repeated the motion, lifting her hair, letting the strands rain down "—this private…pleasure only for me."

His voice was too low for anyone to hear except her. And he was maddening her. Seducing her with only his voice. His fingers running through her hair.

She struggled for composure, but the battle was spiraling out of her control. Her fingers tangled in the fabric of the drapes behind her. She was probably mangling the poor things. Better that than letting her hands go where they wanted to go.

Around Cage. Over him. Everywhere.

She lowered her head, her chin dipping. His fingers found her nape. Stroked. Petted.

He might as well have set a live wire to her spine for the sensations he caused. Was causing.

Oh, dear Lord.

"Cage. We…can't. Lucy—"

"Shh." His voice whispered over her ear, followed immediately by his lips as he nuzzled her earlobe. "Just let me do this. For a minute. Or two. Or twenty." He pulled her hair to the other side, smoothing it down her shoulder. Her arm. Over her breast.

Her heart surged against him and her knees nearly collapsed for the pleasure of it. She was drowning in liquid heat.

Then she felt his mouth on her neck. Heard the timbre of his breathing deepen. She started to lift her hands, to touch him.

"Don't touch me." His lips moved against her throat. "It's safer."

She exhaled shakily. He was drifting his fingers through her hair again. Rearranging it around both shoulders. "Nothing about you is safe," she whispered shakily.

"I'm hardly touching you."

Craning her head around until her lips could find his was proving futile. "What you're touching is making me—"

He stilled, one palm cupping her breast through skeins of hair, the other sliding through loose strands, fingers grazing her nape. "Making you…what?"

She tilted her head back as far as his holds on her hair allowed and looked at him. Full on. Gathered enough strength to speak. Heaven help her, to challenge. "Can't you tell?"

She knew what he'd see. Her cheeks were flushed. Her nipples were so tight they ached. She was trembling from head to foot and all points in-between. Particularly in-between. They were both fully dressed and she'd never been more aroused in her entire life.

She'd never had anyone move her—physically, mentally, emotionally—the way he did. Not even Scott. How would she ever survive if Cage touched more than her *hair?* Just then she didn't think he'd even need to, and wasn't that quite a statement on how much the man affected her?

His lips were parted a little, as if even he was having trouble getting enough air.

It was, she supposed hazily, some small comfort.

"Yeah," he finally said, his voice even lower. "I can see. And I've wanted you looking this way for a while now." He lifted one hand, flattening the drapes as he braced his arm against the window above them. He stepped in another few inches. Until there was no pretending that she wasn't painfully aware of the exquisitely tight fit of his jeans. And the reason why.

"I get only a few hours of sleep at night," he said, "and what I do get is full of this." He pressed gently against her. "Thoughts of you. Me. I'll lie there, hard as a rock, wondering if you're tossing and turning in that squeaky bed because you're thinking—or dreaming—about tossing and turning with me."

She shuddered. His words were too accurate.

He pressed his forehead against hers. She could feel the heat of him, the beat of his heart like some freight train bearing down on them.

Or maybe that was just her blood pulsing through her veins.

"I went into your room last week," he whispered. "You were in the living room with Luce. Working on some math thing you're supposed to be teaching her, but she was practicing piano and I could hear you complaining about the directions in the math book." His fingers strayed to her chin only to slide back toward her ear. Glide through her hair again.

She dissolved a little more. "M-math's not my best subject."

"I was going to oil those springs but good. Not just spray them like I did when you first got to the Lazy-B. But really fix the problem."

She opened her mouth, desperate for some air.

"I didn't oil them," he said. His voice was rougher. "I sat there and stared at that old bed, imagining you lying in it, turning from side to side, the sheets tangling around—between—your legs. Your hair—" he broke off, taking a hissing breath "—your hair spread out all over the pillowcase."

It was as if he'd watched her trying to sleep. Had seen her for himself. Night after night. Week after week. She heard a soft sound, a moan, coming from her throat, and couldn't stop it anymore than she could stop the images he was creating.

Then he twined his fingers in her hair more tightly, tugging back her head until she had to look at him. "Tell me what you dream about at night, Belle. Just tell me. And put me out of my miscry. One way or another."

She stared at him, mute. Words dammed up behind her lips, too many words, too little strength to get them out.

He pressed his mouth to her forehead. Tipped her head back. Sifted her hair again through his fingers, spreading his arms wide, luxuriating in the length and weight of it. It slowly drifted, strand by strand, from his long, calloused fingers. His mouth touched her eyes. Her cheeks. Closed with the same exquisite slowness that his hands exercised, over her mouth. Not taking. Not plundering.

Just…tasting. Reveling.

And he trembled. Because of her.

"I dream about you touching me," she mumbled against his lips. Her entire body felt flushed with prickles of heat.

He exhaled and she breathed him in. He tucked her head against his chest, his shoulders curving around her, a world of their own creation right there in that moment of space. Of time. "I dream about that, too," he murmured. "Me touching you. You touching me. Every little touch causing a soft creak in that bed. Every catching breath causing it to moan a little louder."

She gasped, pressing her head harder against him, grabbing his biceps no matter what he'd warned. She was trembling so violently, her legs were barely holding her. "Stop."

But he didn't. "And always, always this hair of yours, a dark river against the sheets."

His hands returned to her head, sliding around, through, shaping her skull, something that shouldn't have been so exquisitely intimate, yet was. And it was sending her right over the edge. "Cage, you're going to make me…ah—" He covered her mouth with his, swallowing her gasping moan.

Then his lips burned to her ear again. "Let it happen, Belle. Let me have this at least. Let me have a little of what you dream. Of what I dream." He stroked through her hair, again. "Maybe you haven't come in that bed, Belle, but I've imagined it."

She whimpered a little at that. At the appalling bluntness of it. At the seduction of it.

"That's why I didn't oil the springs. I've *wanted* it.

I've wanted to hear those soft, barely noticeable sounds of you in that bed, and I swear on my father's grave that it's only been you that has caused me to think it. Even if it was only in my imagination."

She shook her head, denial, admission, she didn't know what. All she knew was that he was making love to her, and he was doing nothing but touch her head. Getting inside her head. And it was working.

"I want it now," he repeated.

"Kiss me," she begged, nearly broken with need.

He did. His hands fisted in her hair and his mouth covered hers.

Swallowed the keening cry she couldn't manage to contain as she convulsed.

He caught her around the waist, hauling her against him, absorbing the shudders that quaked mindlessly, endlessly, through her there in that private world. And when she finally came to herself again, when they weren't just a mass of sensation, of emotion, when she could form thoughts, he kissed her again, stifling her embarrassment at her own lack of control back into submission.

And after he'd kissed her long and well, he carried her to the burgundy-and-navy plaid couch and sat down, holding her on his lap. Pressed her tight against him for an aching moment, before she felt the effort work through him to relax his hold.

Then he gave a shuddering sigh and threw his head back against the couch. "Thank you."

She could still feel the shape, the length of him pressing hard and insistent against her hip. Her cheeks felt on fire. And embarrassed or not, she couldn't pretend that she didn't want more. "But you haven't—"

He covered her mouth with his hand. "Don't even say it. Trust me." He blew out a measured breath. "Just sit here with me. It'll go away."

She flushed even harder. Tugged his hand away from her mouth, only to tangle her fingers with his and collapse weakly against him.

"Might take a month of Sundays, though," he warned blackly. "Couple of Weaver winters."

She couldn't help it.

She giggled.

His hooded eyes met hers.

And he smiled. Then he laughed. Out loud. From the belly. A laugh that jiggled its way right through her.

And she knew, in all of her life, she might never hear a more beautiful sound.

Chapter Fourteen

Eventually—when Belle had regained enough muscle and mind control to attempt simple functions—she used Cage's SUV to drive back to Nikki's place. But it had been wrenching to leave him.

Smart, definitely. But nevertheless wrenching.

She still felt the ache of it when she let herself in with her key, only to choke back a scream.

But it was only her sister sitting there in the living room, hunched over a book in the corner of her enormous couch.

Nikki eyed her for a moment, her blue eyes speculative. "I hope you've come back to clean up the mess you left in my closet."

After everything, Belle had completely forgotten about that. "I will. Thanks for the dress, by the way."

"I hope you at least cut off the tags before you wore

it. It looks better on you than me, actually. Keep it. Your closet will rejoice, I'm sure."

Belle dropped her purse on the coffee table and sat down in front of her sister. Grabbed the book out of Nikki's hands and folded them between her own. "Are you all right?"

Nikki sighed a little. Tilted her auburn head to the side and studied Belle right back. "Are you?"

She swallowed a little, but kept her composure intact. "I will be once you tell me what's going on."

"By the looks of it, I'd say you've been playing truth or dare with someone. Since I know you are beyond being over Scott, it must be Cage Buchanan. Truth?"

Maybe her cheeks were a little rosy from Cage's five o'clock shadow, but she knew she didn't look as if she'd just climbed from bed.

They'd never made it to the bed.

Her face went a little hotter at that. It would be a long while before she could think about it without being shocked at her own behavior. At the outrageous and unrelenting way Cage had played her. And she'd sung.

And she wasn't sure she'd be able to sleep in that squeaky bed back at the Lazy-B again. She just might have to sleep on the floor.

"I was with Cage," she admitted. "*And* Lucy."

Nikki eyed her.

"Well. Lucy was asleep in the other room," she admitted grudgingly. Then gave herself a hard, mental shake. "They gave me a ride down here to see *you*. My Jeep is currently kaput."

"Because it's only a hundred years old."

"Not everyone drives around the latest models," Belle countered lightly, "the way you do. So. Talk."

Her sister swallowed. "I'm pregnant."

Belle waited.

Nikki pushed to her feet, shoving a shaking hand through her thick, auburn hair. "You'd think I'd get used to hearing those words come out of my mouth, wouldn't you? I'm pregnant. I'm pregnant." She shook her head. "Nope. Still freaks me out." Her smile wavered.

Belle hopped up and wrapped her arms around her sister.

"Do you love him? This guy? The one you're not ready to talk about?"

"Do you love *him?* Cage?" Nikki's whisper was ragged.

Belle swallowed hard. But this was her sister. The one with whom she'd shared their mother's womb. They were twins. Different. Alike. But always honest.

"I'm afraid I'm starting to," she admitted. "I can't even imagine going back to Huffington, and that's—" She shook her head, unable to explain. "But I want to know about *you.*"

Nikki sighed heavily. She pushed Belle back and studied her face for a moment. "Later. For now sleep or chocolate?"

Nikki had always been an independent soul. "Chocolate," Belle declared. Sooner or later her sister would talk. "Most definitely."

Nikki turned toward the kitchen, padding along in her bare feet. "Fortunately, in the chocolate area, I'm well prepared."

They ended up falling asleep on the couch facing

each other, the carton of Double Chocolate Fudge Madness empty on the bare inch of cushion not covered by their sprawling legs.

Belle woke first and watched her sister sleeping.

Nikki was going to be a mother.

She pressed her palms flat against her own abdomen, as she wondered what it felt like. Not the worry over being a single mom, but what it felt like to have something—a new creation—growing inside.

But thinking about that naturally led to thinking about how one became pregnant, which naturally led to thinking about Cage, which naturally led to Belle not having any hope of going back to sleep.

So she carefully slid off the enormous couch. Nikki sank down a little more, unconsciously taking advantage of the extra space just the way she'd always done whenever she and Belle had had to share the back seat of their family car.

Belle draped an ivory afghan over her sister and plucked the empty ice-cream carton off the couch. Silently gathered up the spoons and napkins and carried it all into the kitchen, tidying up. She flicked on the coffeemaker, then went upstairs, took a quick shower, and changed into the spare outfit she'd brought.

Then she cleaned up the mess—which admittedly was more mammoth than she'd thought—of clothes she'd left when she'd raided Nik's closet the night before.

She left a thermal mug of decaffeinated coffee on the table beside Nikki, and with a matching one in her own hand, let herself out of the house, locked it behind her and drove back to the hotel. She buzzed Cage's room from the lobby as he'd suggested she do before she'd left him the night before.

He and Lucy arrived within twenty minutes.

It wasn't taxing to wait. The hotel had that pretty pool, after all. And plenty of chairs around it that weren't yet occupied at the early hour.

She had her coffee. She had the beautiful promise of an early Sunday morning, with a sky that couldn't be more perfectly blue, and clouds that couldn't be more perfectly like big, squishy cotton balls. She had a year's supply of chocolate circulating in her bloodstream and the certainty that her sister—while still reeling—was, bottom line, as strong as she'd ever been.

And she had the sound of Cage's laughter in her heart.

Lucy swung into view first, her freshly washed hair lying over her shoulders in twin braids. She waved and aimed toward Belle, plopping down onto a chair with no sign of the stiffness she'd exhibited the night before.

Cage followed more slowly, a foam cup eclipsed by his long fingers.

She gulped her coffee, dragging her eyes away from his fingers. And nearly choked on the liquid.

Served her right for thinking *those* thoughts about his wonderfully shaped, perfectly masculine hands.

He gave a crooked smile and sat down in the third chair, setting his coffee cup on the table where his fingers hovered around the rim. He lifted his other hand, and she realized he'd been carrying a blueberry muffin. "Want one?" She shook her head and he handed the muffin to Lucy. "Ever catch up to your sister?"

"She was there when I got back last night."

"And?"

"And…I feel better. Thanks a lot for driving me. Really."

He lifted his coffee, the faintest sketch of a toast in his movement. "My pleasure."

Well. She nervously tugged her ponytail over her shoulder. When his gaze shifted a little, she hurriedly pushed it back behind her shoulder and tucked her hands beneath her legs on the chair. "So. Any preferences for breakfast?"

Cage just looked at her.

Fresh heat streaked through her.

She focused on Lucy and it took no small effort to do so. "Well? What are your druthers, miss? Waffles? Eggs?"

"If we go to Grandma's care center, we could have breakfast there. They always have a huge Sunday buffet. That's what we usually do. Right, Dad? Then we can introduce Belle to her."

Belle absorbed that. She looked at Cage, who had begun studying the contents of his coffee cup. "Yes," he said after a moment. Then his gaze lifted and focused once more on Belle. "Let Belle decide."

Lucy looked hopefully at her.

Belle would have preferred to go anyplace else. She'd have preferred to drive straight to the moon and back rather than go to the care center.

All of which only proved that a coward still lurked beneath her skin. "A *huge* buffet?" she questioned Lucy. "Huge in relation to what? To the number of history papers you've written in the past eight weeks? To the number of birds congregating in that tree over there, hoping you leave some crumbs of your muffin behind?"

Lucy laughed, delightedly. "They have, like, five kinds of eggs. And I *know* you like eggs."

Belle smiled and tugged on Lucy's braid. "So I do," she admitted.

So, after Cage took care of the checkout, they drove across town to the pretty tree-shrouded facility where Cage's mother lived.

Belle's eyes took in every corner. Every sight and sound and smell. She'd feared the place would be unbearably institutional. But it wasn't. It was more like a sprawling, gracious home. The front door was double width and could accommodate wheelchairs, but it was a far cry from some sliding metal-and-glass monstrosity that so many places possessed. Inside, there were plants everywhere. The staff members weren't wearing starched whites.

Cage and Lucy headed down a hall, obviously familiar faces from the greetings they received. The exclamations of how well Lucy was maneuvering with her crutches since the last time they'd been there.

Belle would have followed behind them, but Cage slowed up a little until she walked *with* him.

At least he didn't pretend that this was something either one of them could have predicted when she'd become Lucy's PT.

After a couple turns of corridors lined with lovely artwork and occasional chairs, Lucy stopped in front of an open door. She barely knocked before unceremoniously entering. "Hi, Grandma."

Belle swallowed and hung back. She was used to working with people in all manner of physical conditions. She didn't know exactly what Mrs. Buchanan's condition was, but she knew with certainty that no amount of training could have prepared her for this moment.

And Cage, no matter what, couldn't possibly want her here.

The man she'd thought she'd known these past months surely would be affronted by her very presence here.

But he gave no indication of anything. Unlike the previous night in his hotel room when he'd been excruciatingly verbal, his thoughts now were far too well contained.

Lucy had no similar affliction. She pointed the tip of her crutch at Belle, startling the life out of her.

Belle grabbed Cage's arm. "Look."

"What?"

"Lucy took a step without her crutches," she hissed under her breath. "She's standing on her own."

And the girl had. She was. She continued gesturing with her crutch, an extension of her hand, for Belle to come closer. "Come in and meet my grandma," she urged.

Belle blindly walked into the room. She was still amazed at what Lucy was doing so unconsciously. Fortunately, too amazed to say something that might send Lucy backtracking. And she found herself facing Cage Buchanan's mother.

She was sitting in a side chair, next to a small round table, a book on her lap. A mystery. Belle instinctively knew without having to look closely that the stack of books on the bookshelf beneath the window held books by the same authors that filled the shelves at the Lazy-B. The books Cage read.

The window was open and a slight breeze billowed gently through the delicate white curtains, lightly stirring the bronzy curls of the woman.

She was beautiful. More than the aging black-and-white photos hanging in the house at the Lazy-B could ever have predicted.

A female version of the beautiful son she'd borne. The same color hair, the same breathtakingly clear blue eyes. Her skin was soft, nearly unlined. She wore a simple, pink sheath-style dress. Her feet were tucked into delicate pink pumps. She could have been a perfectly healthy woman dressed for church.

"This is my friend, Belle Day." Lucy introduced her cheerfully.

Belle held her breath. But Cage's mother merely slid her softly smiling gaze from Lucy to Belle's face. Obviously, to her Belle's last name was just a name. Her breath leaked out. She stepped forward, holding out her hand. "Hello, Mrs. Buchanan."

"How nice of you to bring Lucy," she said, squeezing Belle's hand with both of hers. They were soft. Cool. Utterly gentle. Only a close ear would have noticed the halting tempo of her speech. And Belle felt a faint smile on her own lips in return of the one directed so sweetly at her.

Then Mrs. Buchanan looked beyond Belle at Cage. She reached out her hands to him, perfectly friendly. "And who would you be?"

Knowing that his own mother didn't recognize him was one thing. Witnessing it another.

The sadness of it was encompassing. Wide and deep. Belle kept her smile in place only through sheer effort as she watched Cage step forward.

He leaned down, holding her hands, and kissed his mother's cheek.

His knuckles were white.

Belle wanted to look away, but couldn't.

"Hi, Mom." His voice held only gentleness. "We came to have breakfast with you, so I hope you haven't already been down to the dining room."

The woman nodded easily. Cage's greeting had no more effect on her than Belle's had. "I was reading. And nearly forgot to eat." She laughed a little, realizing the book had fallen to the floor and took it when Cage handed it to her. She set it on the table, then rose. She smoothed her hand over Lucy's head, pure delight in the gesture. "You look very nice today, Lucy. Are you getting taller?"

"I'm a teenager now, Grandma. My birthday was two days ago." Lucy swung through the doorway. "Maybe I'm taller 'cause of these tennis shoes I'm wearing. They look cool, don't they? Belle gave 'em to me. For some reason, she thinks I like pink. Do you think they'll have blueberry waffles this week? I really missed them when we were here last time."

Belle watched them go, Lucy's cheerful chatter so natural and unaffected, floating down the hall as they went.

Cage stood beside her. He touched her arm through the filmy sleeve of her blouse. "Are you okay?"

She looked up at him. That he could ask *her* that, when it should be she posing the question to him…she shook her head a little. "I'm so sorry, Cage."

"So am I."

She pressed her fingers to her lips for a moment. Felt the drift of the air through the window. "You know, after the accident, my dad was never the same. He wasn't hurt. Not physically. But…he just wasn't the same."

Cage's lips twisted, but he said nothing.

"He had a massive heart attack three years later. I was sixteen. But sometimes I think he left his heart on the highway that night."

"You still had your mother. Your sister," he said after a moment.

"And you had no one." Her eyes blurred. No family at all. And there was no question that family meant everything to this man. It had just taken her a while to see it. "Your mother—"

"Traumatic brain injury," he said evenly. "The only person since the accident that she remembers from one day to the next is Lucy. We don't know why. Maybe because I've been bringing Lucy here since she was born. My mother functions well. Her speech is good. Her motor functions are good. But she wouldn't remember to look before crossing a street. She wouldn't remember to take off her shoes before getting into bed. She wouldn't remember that a sharp knife would cut her hand."

The tears flowed down Belle's cheeks.

"I took her back to the Lazy-B once. Lucy was five." His gaze turned inward. "The insurance settlement had run out and I wanted her home. Thought it might help. But she never connected. And whether or not I wanted to admit it, I couldn't help her. She needed to be in a safe environment. The ranch wasn't it." He glanced around the room. The walls were a pale pink, so similar to Lucy's at the Lazy-B. Everything about the room was pretty and soft and feminine. "So I sold nearly everything I owned except the ranch and brought her back."

And Belle knew that it had broken his heart.

"It's my fault."

"Right." His expression was plain. He blamed her father. He always had. Even though no fault had ever been officially declared. Gus Day had walked away from the accident, and Cage's family had not.

"I wanted to go on a winter break with a friend of mine from school. They were going to Mexico for a week. And I wanted to go along in the worst imaginable way. I was thirteen and I thought Cheyenne was about the most boring place on the planet, and Mexico—" she shook her head "—well I knew it wouldn't be boring. But my father said I couldn't go, and my mother—as usual— agreed with him. He didn't like my friend's parents, you see. He thought they were…irresponsible. I thought they were a hoot. More like friends than parents."

"Belle—"

"Let me finish this, Cage." She had to finish. If she didn't now, she wasn't sure she ever could. And face-to-face with the reality of what he'd been left with that night grieved her so deeply, she knew she couldn't live with herself if she *didn't*.

No matter if it meant he'd never look at her the same again. He deserved the truth. All of it.

"My father was right, of course, but I learned that only after a while. They were busted for some stuff. Anyway." She knew she was babbling. Tried to focus.

"You don't have to cry about this, Belle. I don't blame you for what happened that night. Maybe I started out that way—hell, I know I did. I resented the fact that you and your sister grew up having what had been ripped away from me."

"But I am to blame," she burst out. "The trip to Mexico. I was determined to go, you see. And Daddy just kept telling me I couldn't go. And I told him that I hated him and would *never* forgive him, and stormed out of the house. I went to my friend's and, even though her parents had to have known I didn't have permission to go, we all headed out of town."

Despite her tears she could see his expression had gone still. Stoic. And her heart broke. For him. For the past. For the future.

"Dad caught up to us after twenty miles," she went on. Pushing the words past the vise of her throat. "If it was even that far. I wanted to crawl in a hole and die of embarrassment when he made the van pull over. Now, I think it was surprising he hadn't just sent the police after us. We were driving back to Cheyenne when the accident happened. I was so angry. I wouldn't even sit in the front with him. I was ignoring him. Lying in the back seat like some...some spoiled child."

She pressed her eyes shut. "If my dad was distracted, if he wasn't paying enough attention, if it *was* his fault, then it was because of me. And even if it wasn't his fault, if it was just the ice, or the snow, or whatever the way I was always told, it was still because of me. Don't you see?" She opened her eyes again and faced Cage. "We were only out that night, because of me."

Chapter Fifteen

Belle stood there, feeling as brittle as the last autumn leaf. Waiting for him to look at her again, for his eyes to go cold and flat. For him to tell her that she'd interfered in his life enough, to get the hell away from his family and stay away. Far, far away.

"Why are you telling me this?"

She stared down at her hands. She *had* helped Lucy. She knew she had. Knowingly or not, the girl had stood squarely on both feet and taken a step without the aid of her crutches. It didn't mean the job was done. But it meant that Belle had helped. Finally.

"Belle."

She lifted her chin and looked up at him, wanting to memorize his face. *Him.* From the top of his bronzed head, over the cobalt-blue shirt that made his eyes even more startling, to the bottom of his black boots. A different pair than what he wore around the ranch. These were newer. Shined.

Because he'd known he was visiting his mother, even though she wouldn't remember him from one week to the next.

"Because I...I'm falling in love with you," she said. And she'd told him the one thing sure to put an end to whatever possibilities might exist for them. "Because you have a right to at least blame the right person." She wiped her cheeks and turned to leave.

He caught her wrist.

The pain sweeping through her was physical. Nearly sending her to her knees. But she stood there, knowing the pain he'd endured—was still enduring every time he came to this comfortable room where his mother's life was contained—eclipsed hers by legions.

"Do you mean that?"

Confusion made her hesitate.

"That you love me," he said impatiently.

Did he want his pound of flesh, then? If it made him feel better, he could have it. And more. "Yes." What was the point of recanting?

A muscle worked in his jaw, more noticeable because his face was pale beneath the tan he'd earned putting in alone the work of ten men on the Lazy-B.

Her wrist was beginning to ache beneath his shackling grip. But she'd have done anything just then to take every ounce of pain he felt inside herself, if only to ease him, somehow.

Then his fingers—as deliberate now as they'd been the night before when he'd sat them on the couch, both of them wanting *more* than they could have in that hotel room—carefully eased their tight hold. He lifted her hand, his eyes downcast.

"Maybe it's time to leave the past in the past," he said, his voice sliding over her, deep and gruff.

"The past isn't bringing Lucy here week after week to visit your mother." It was his present, and his future.

He let out a long, deep breath. "No," he agreed. "But Lucy's happy. My mother is happy. She doesn't know anything else now. She's content. This is what *is*."

He slid his hand behind Belle's neck, tipping her face up. Everything inside her gathered into a hard knot centered somewhere under her heart. He lowered his head, pressed his forehead to hers, eyes shut.

Hot tears burned down Belle's cheeks. She cautiously touched his shoulders. Her fingertips trembling along his neck. Feeling the tension inside him. Not daring to believe that he wasn't pushing her away.

"Maybe it's time I let myself be happy with what is, too."

A shudder of grief was working through her shoulders, no matter how hard she tried to suppress it.

Then his fingers slid under her chin, lifting it and his mouth covered hers, swallowing her hiccuping sob. "Don't cry," he muttered. "I can't take it."

A statement that only had the opposite effect. Belle buried her face against the front of his shirt. He swore under his breath, tugged her over to the chair where his mother had been sitting and sat down, arranging Belle in his lap as easily as if she were smaller than Lucy. His shoulder moved, then he was handing her a tissue he'd plucked from the box on the bookcase.

But the tears just kept coming and he moved again,

and she felt the cardboard cube being pushed into her hands.

"Go to it, then," he said gruffly.

She leaned against him, sliding her arm over his shoulder, holding him. The box crumpled between them. His hand moved down her back. Back up again.

And after a long while, Belle felt an odd sort of peace creep through her. She sat back a little. Mopped her face with tissues. Finally looked up into that gaze of his. "What do we do now?"

He was silent for a moment. His fingers toyed with the length of her ponytail, pulling it over her shoulder. And even though her emotions were fully spent, the action felt as if he was spreading a layer of soft warmth over her. "We go have breakfast," he finally said. "And then we go home to the ranch."

She absorbed that. Nodded a little. Step-by-step. "And then?"

"Then we'll see what happens."

"You, um, you still want me to work with Lucy?" Her voice was shaking again.

"Yes."

"Okay." It was more than she could have expected.

"I want you to work with me."

"On...what?"

He leaned over her, catching her softly parted lips between his. First the lower. Then the upper. "Learning how not to be an ogre."

"You're not an ogre," she assured thickly. And hoping that she wasn't making the biggest misstep of all, she pressed her mouth against his.

His arms tightened around her.

"Whoa. Wowzer. No *wonder* you guys are taking so long!"

Belle yanked back at the exclamation. Her lips felt as puffy as her eyes. Her ponytail was askew.

"Caught in the act," Cage muttered against the shell of Belle's ear. She was blushing like a spring rose and he looked past her to his daughter, gaping at them as if she'd just discovered fire or something. "We'll be along in a minute, Luce."

Her eyes were bright. No surprise there. She adored Belle. But he was a little surprised that she didn't seem more shocked. Her head bobbed and she planted her crutches, turning smartly only to take another quick look back at them, a grin already on her face. "Wow," she said again. Then swung right out of sight again.

Belle was scrambling off his lap. "Maybe you should go talk to her, or, or something."

"About what? You think she doesn't know what a kiss is all about? She already told me you made sure she knew the facts of life after she got her period."

Belle gulped a little and looked away. "Well, I wasn't sure you were up to—"

"I told you. Luce has always been able to talk to me." But damned if he hadn't been more than a little relieved when he *had* cornered his girl after that particular episode. Not that they hadn't discussed the facts of life long before then. Lucy was a rancher's daughter, for cripes sake. She knew how babies came to be.

But it was one thing when it was talking about puppies or calving. It was another thing entirely when it was his *daughter*.

"I'm always underestimating you," Belle said quietly. "Aren't I? I'm sorry."

"For caring about my daughter?"

"I love her, too."

He let the fact of it settle inside him, only to have to acknowledge that it wasn't all that much of a surprise, after all.

"Come on," he said, taking up her hand in his. "Breakfast."

Her fingers slid through his, holding tightly.

And they went to breakfast.

Later that afternoon, Cage dropped Belle off at her house in town since there still was the matter of her Jeep to be seen to. The dropping off took longer than it might have, since Lucy was curious to see where Belle lived, necessitating a brief tour.

By the time Cage and Lucy drove off again, Belle knew that Brenda Wyatt had gotten quite an eyeful, hovering obviously out in her front yard. No way could she have failed to miss the kiss Cage planted on her before climbing into his truck and driving on down the road.

By the time Belle had thrown a hasty load of laundry into the wash and tracked down the whereabouts of her Jeep, her mother was standing on her front step, knocking on the door before unceremoniously letting herself in.

Gloria Clay propped her hands on her slender hips and tilted her auburn head that was only showing a few strands of silver. Her blue eyes were expectant. "Well? Has your phone stopped working? Where have you been all weekend? And *what* is going on with your sister? She's harder to get hold of than you are."

Belle warily dumped the towels she'd taken from the dryer on the couch and sat down beside them. "I went down to Cheyenne." She reached for a towel and spread it out, taking inordinate care over the folds.

Her mother lifted an eyebrow. "And?"

"And nothing. Well. I met Cage Buchanan's mother." The admission came out fast. She felt as if she was ten years old again and she and Nik had been caught sneaking Christmas cookie dough out of the fridge.

"Oh. My." The news was enough to distract Gloria for a moment, but Belle didn't hold out much hope it would last. Gloria sat on the other side of the towels and grabbed one, smartly flipping it into a perfect fold in a fraction of the time it took Belle. Then she rested her folded hands on top of the fluffy terry cloth. "Is she doing well?"

Belle wasn't sure how she'd expected her mother to react. "She looked lovely."

Gloria made a soft *mmm.* "What's going on, Annabelle?"

"Brenda Wyatt didn't give you the skinny?" She finished folding and stacked the towels together. Then wished she hadn't finished so quickly.

Her mother waved a hand. "As if I care what nonsense that woman spouts. She's been gossiping since long before either one of us came to Weaver. Managed to cause all that fuss Tristan and Hope had to deal with when that reporter came snooping for a story about him." She tilted her head a little. "Of course, that all had a rather nice result in the end since they got married because of it and fell in love. Hope's expecting again, you know. Erik's over four now. We were all beginning to wonder if he was going to get a little brother or sister "

A quick rush of pleasure jolted through Belle, right along with a sturdy helping of guilt for keeping silent about Nikki's news. "I didn't know. That's great."

Her mother's blue gaze rested on Belle's head for a moment. "Well. Sawyer told me about your Jeep."

"It's been hauled to the garage."

Gloria held out her hand and dropped a key into Belle's. "You can borrow this until yours is running again."

"Mom—"

"Don't argue, now. Squire insisted and you know what *he's* like. There're plenty of vehicles to spare around the Double-C. You can leave it off again next week at Angel's party if yours is done by then. And none of us has to worry about you driving that old thing on those roads out to the Lazy-B. I know it was your father's, sweetheart, but even he wouldn't expect you to drive it forever."

Belle shrugged. "I like the Jeep, Mom."

Gloria nodded. "So, does this man mean something to you, or are you just using him to get over that fool, Scott? That boy had no integrity at all, proposing the way he did when he already had a wife. And *then* blaming you because he didn't recover as fast as he wanted to."

"My feelings for Cage have nothing to do with Scott," she assured. "I can't believe I ever thought what I felt for him was love." Or let him convince her she wasn't a good enough therapist to help *anyone*.

"Because you know what real love feels like now?"

Belle pulled the stack of towels onto her lap. Put them back on the table. Rose and paced. "What really happened that night, Mom? The accident. Whose fault was it?"

Gloria watched her, a hint of sympathy in her eyes. "Accidents can happen with no one being at fault, darling. And that night was icy. Your father did feel responsible, though. Which is why—"

"Why what?"

But Gloria just shook her head. "Nothing. It's in the past."

The past. "I told Cage why we were out there that night at all."

"I see."

Belle suddenly sank down on the coffee table. "I'm falling for him, Mom. And Lucy. And that brick house with its antiquated furniture and everything."

"And how does Cage feel about you?"

"He doesn't seem to hate me." A miracle she still had trouble believing.

Gloria lifted her eyebrow again. "Is that all?"

She was too old to be blushing, yet she did. "Maybe not. I don't know."

"I imagine you do, but you don't have to tell me all the details," Gloria assured her wryly. "My heart won't be able to take it. Now. It's getting to be supper time. Squire wants ribs from Colby's. Everyone's meeting over there. The entire family. Newt is saving the back room because we'll need all the space to fit. You'll join us."

There was no question in it.

"Where is Squire?"

"Right here, girl," the tall man said, stepping through

the door. He wasn't quite as tall as his five sons, but his iron-gray head ducked a little anyway as he entered. A habit she'd noticed more than once in her stepbrothers, who'd undoubtedly conked their heads on low doorways often enough to be conditioned. "Was just checking the rain gutters on the side of your house. One of 'em is coming loose. If that man of yours doesn't come back to town this week to get it fixed up, I'll have one of the boys come over and take care of it."

Belle just shook her head a little and reached up to hug him. There was no more stopping Squire than there was any of the Clays. The "boys" he'd referred to were all grown men, and gossip in town must have been plentiful indeed if people were already calling Cage "her man."

Once she'd spent a few hours in their company over a half-dozen tables pushed together in Colby's back room to accommodate the mass of Clays who seemed to keep filtering in—she stopped counting after twenty—she felt as if she'd filled up some wellspring inside of her.

That was what family could do.

After supper, while everyone was still passing out hugs and chattering a mile a minute, Belle decided she was not going to wait until morning to go back to the Lazy-B. She had a car—maybe not her beloved Jeep—and no desire whatsoever to sleep in the house of Hope's that she'd been using and every desire to be at the Lazy-B. No matter which bedroom she used.

But her plans were preempted by the sight of Cage, sitting on her front porch.

Her heart kicked hard against her ribs as she climbed

out from the back seat of Sawyer's SUV. She was hardly aware of what she said to him, just that she was relieved when he wheeled around and drove back up the street to collect his own family before going home.

She watched Cage stand. He doffed his brown cowboy hat and his hair gleamed a little under the glow from the porch light. He was twenty yards away yet she could feel the intensity of his gaze.

Tension slipped up her spine, fiery pinpricks careened through her nerves. She couldn't seem to draw enough oxygen into her lungs and her mouth ran dry. She moistened her lips, torn between fleeing or standing her ground. But her rooted feet took the decision from her because she couldn't seem to move to save her soul.

And then he took a step toward her. And another. And there was nothing but purpose in his movements, purpose that no amount of pretense could hide.

Her heart climbed up into her throat.

Closer now. She could see the flame in his eyes, otherworldly pale, blue fire. "Luce is over at Emmy's," he said bluntly. "All night."

"Oh."

"You gonna stand there all night?"

"Maybe." She swallowed. "I can't seem to make my feet move."

"Where were you?"

As if he had every right to know. It didn't occur to her to prevaricate. Or even to challenge. "Colby's. The whole family was there. I was going to drive out to the ranch tonight," she admitted in a rush.

"The Double-C?"

She shook her head.

"The Lazy-B."

She nodded.

"Whose car?" He jerked his chin toward the sexy little convertible sitting in front of the house.

"A spare from Mom and Squire."

"I'm glad." He stepped closer. "Was wondering about it." His voice was low. Quiet. "Like I wondered about that white shirt."

"There's no man but you." The admission felt as momentous as dropping a boulder into a still, still pond. And she wasn't at all certain how high the ripples might roll. Or, even if she were brave enough to find out. "You've had a lot of driving today. Cheyenne. Back and forth to Weaver. You must be tired."

"Inside?"

She pressed her hands down the sides of her jeans. Then nodded and willed her feet to move, heading up the small porch ahead of him. Fumbled with the lock and then the door. He finally reached around her and shoved it open, then nudged her through, and closed the door with a slam, turning and pressing her back against it, his body imprinting itself against hers.

She went straight past wary to aching. No line, no waiting. "I always wondered what swooning was like," she mumbled, staring blindly up as his weight pinned her. "I, um, I guess you're not that tired after all."

"Evidently." His fingers were busy on the tiny black buttons of her blouse then his hands swept inside, finding nothing but bare skin and the world seemed to stop spinning.

Her eyes nearly rolled back in her head. "Good," she

gasped. She tore at his shirt. Made a mess of it since she
got it off his shoulders but not his arms. The crispy
swirl of black hair sprinkling his chest abraded her
breasts. The contrasts between them were inciting. De-
licious.

And then she felt the tease of his tongue along her
lower lip, and the world wasn't still at all. It was racing, spinning, and the only steady port was Cage.

She shuddered, her fingers clenching his corded forearms. Her clothing provided no protection whatsoever
against his searing heat. And, oh, she didn't want to be
protected. She ran her hands up his arms, fumbling over
folds of cobalt shirt, pressed her fingers into the unyielding biceps, her head falling back at his drugging on-
slaught. His breath was harsh when he finally lifted his
head a few inches, hauling in a ragged gulp of air.

"I didn't expect you to happen." His mouth found her
temple. Slid down her jaw.

"I know," her voice was woefully faint. Her fingers
walked up his shoulders. Felt the cords of his neck. She
felt the brush of silky bronze hair against her chin as his
kiss burned along her shoulder blade. Pressed against
the pulse beating frantically in her throat. "I didn't, either."

"Don't talk," he murmured, straightening. He tilted
her head to suit him. "Just kiss me again."

So she did.

She kissed him until her head spun, until her skin felt
molten, and her blood sang. She kissed him until she
couldn't think, until the only thing she knew was the
shape of him, the taste of him. Until she went beyond

fear that kissing him would never be enough to certainty that the fear was irrelevant.

His hands raced over her only to stop and tarry, maddening her with the graze of his calloused fingertips along the bare skin of her back, her abdomen. He lifted his head, and she was conscious enough to flush at the moans rising in her throat when his gaze ran over her, only to stall at the thrust of her rigid nipples through the loosened blouse. His hand slowly drifted from her shoulder, over the push of her breasts against the fabric. His fingertip slid in tightening circles around her nipple, and if it wasn't for his other arm around her waist, her knees would have failed her completely. Then he dragged his finger over the peak, and the sensation was so exquisitely intense, she cried out.

His gaze slashed back to hers as he repeated the motion. She shuddered, mouthing his name.

He exhaled roughly, and covered her mouth again, kissing her deeply. She felt his fingers slide beneath the blouse again, drawing it down, past her shoulders. Off her arms where it floated to their feet. Then his palms covered her flesh.

Belle gasped at the sensations battering her from all sides. His drugging mouth on hers. His clever hands touching her. The unyielding wall of his chest against her. "Hold on," he muttered. Then he simply lifted her off her feet. Her pulse stuttered and she twined her arms around him, burying her face in the curve of his neck. He tasted hot, slightly salty, totally male, and at the flicker of her tongue against him, his grip tightened and his stride faltered. He muttered something under his breath, then moved again. He carried her down the hall. "Where?"

"End of the hall."

His mouth covered hers. Her legs bumped the wall. He swore. She laughed softly. Then he was moving again, turning sideways through the doorway to her bedroom. And even though they were the only ones in the house, he kicked the door shut behind him.

The abrupt slam of wood rocked through her as he let her legs swing down. Closed in her bedroom. Why did it feel more intimate just because he'd closed the door? She shivered.

His hands cupped her face. Calloused thumb slowly brushing the corner of her lips. "Say no now, Belle."

She wanted to feel the hard press of his chest again against her breasts, but he held himself away, touching only her face. "Is that what you want me to do? Say no?" Moonlight shafted through her windows, painting the corner of her bed in its tender light. She reached up, unable to resist, and pressed her palm against the muscle flexing in his jaw. "Are you already regretting this, then?"

"No." He lowered his forehead, pressing it against hers. "But you can still change your mind. Now. If you do later…" His voice was low. Rough.

Her palm slid to his nape, fingers slipping through his silky hair. "I'm not changing my mind." Stretching up, she brushed her cheek along his. Whispered in his ear. "Not now. Not later." Not ever, she feared.

He exhaled sharply, and in less than a breath, there was no space for even a whisper between them as he turned to her bed. Settled her in the center of it. She felt the kiss of air on her abdomen in the moment before his lips displaced it as he drew down her jeans. It was like being dipped in fire. She scrabbled at his shoulders, but he caught her hands in his, fingers sliding between fingers, palms meeting palms.

"Let me." His lips brushed her thigh.

And then she wasn't being dipped in fire, the conflagration came from the inside out. Only when she was gasping, then crying out his name, did he slowly work his way upward. She knew she was shaking, but couldn't seem to bring order to her senses, couldn't seem to grasp anything solid or real, except him.

He caught her nipple between his lips, teeth scraping oh-so-gently. His thigh, hair-roughened and hard, notched between her legs. When had he gotten rid of the rest of his clothes?

Then his mouth slid along the column of her neck. His breath was rough. His heartbeat pulsing hard against hers. He slid one hand behind her knee, urging it higher against his hip and groaned softly as his flesh tantalized hers.

She arched, greedy for so much more, and he laughed softly, turning until she lay over him. She arched against him, so much emotion inside her that she feared she might never recover. "I need you," she whispered.

He went curiously still. "Do you?"

If there were any places inside her that hadn't been softened beyond hope where he was concerned, his tense, urgent expression found them. Her throat went tight. Her fingertips grazed the sharp lines of his jaw, her palm cradled his cheek. "Yes."

She could feel the muscle flexing in his jaw. Feel every muscle he possessed seeming to gather itself. Her heart sped, the world spun as he pulled her beneath him.

"Remember that," he said. His fingers fumbled with her ponytail, and then he was spreading her hair out around her. And when he was done, he found her mouth as he took her. Unerring. True.

She pressed her head back against the bed, hauling in a keening breath, feeling her emotions stripped bare. Wanting the moment never to end, wanting to hide from it forever.

He breathed a soft oath that sounded more like a plea. Her fingers curled, but he pressed his hands against her arms, smoothing upward until his palms met hers. Fingers linked. "Open your eyes," he whispered.

Such a simple act. It took all her strength. She looked at him. At the naked desire burning in his eyes, in the tendons standing out of his neck, his shoulders. Pleasure flooded through her and she shuddered wildly, on the precipice of something deeper, stronger than she could have ever suspected. Her fingertips dug into his hands. And he moved again.

"Next time," he promised roughly, "I'm going to make this last all day."

She laughed, but the sound was thick, and helpless tears leaked from the corners of her eyes.

He made a soft sound, almost *tsking,* and drew their linked hands closer to her head, where he caught the moisture with his thumbs. His movements were suddenly, indescribably gentle. "What? Did I hurt you?"

She shook her head. "I feel you...in...my heart."

Her voice shook. She pressed mindlessly against him. "Don't stop," she begged.

"Not possible." He kissed her again, conquering her mouth as surely as he conquered her body. Then he tore his mouth from hers, his breath harsh, and the sight of him, muscles cording, eyes hot with need, sent her that last, infinitesimal distance and she went screaming into the abyss.

He went with her.

Chapter Sixteen

Belle tucked her hand beneath her cheek and lay quietly in her bed.

Early-dawn light was sneaking through the window, slowly creeping over the foot of the bed and the tangle of sheets and blanket. Any minute, she expected Cage to wake.

But for now, for now she watched him sleep. As he'd been sleeping for hours.

His hair was tousled. His lashes thick and dark and still. There was no tension coiled in his long, strong body. There was only sleep.

It was a sight to behold, Belle thought. And difficult not to touch him. Not to let her hands drift over his wide shoulder. Sift through the hair on his chest and feel the slow, easy rise and fall of his breathing.

She didn't touch him, though. Didn't want to break his slumber.

So her eyes traveled where her hands dared not. Her body, aching in unaccustomed places, her senses, still alive from the feelings he'd wrought absorbed the close warmth of him.

What the future held for them was a mystery. We'll see what happens, he'd said.

She wanted to believe that left an open vista of hope. Needed to believe it. Her gaze drifted over his hand, thrown above his head, fingers lax. Palm exposed. His bicep, a perfect relief.

She closed her eyes, exhaling slowly. There was no objectivity in her appreciation of his male beauty. She couldn't admire him without wanting to touch him.

But he was sleeping. Soundly and undisturbed for the first time in Lord only knew how long. She carefully turned on her back. Then her other side. Gave the small clock sitting on her nightstand a baleful look and turned her face into her pillow. Another few hours and Cage would be wanting to collect Lucy. Champing at the bit to get back to the Lazy-B and the chores that waited for no man's weekend away.

Cage shifted. "Too far away." His voice was husky, full of sleep. A long arm slid around her from behind, easily removing the six inches of space separating them. She sucked in an absurdly needful breath as his hand flattened across her abdomen, pressing her back against him before sliding up and covering her breast. His chest felt hot against her spine and everywhere that she was soft, he was…not.

She snuck a glance up at him, but his eyes were still closed.

She attempted to do the same.

"Quit wiggling," he said after a moment.

Forget another hour of *z's*. "I can't help it," she whispered. "I'm not used to this."

His thumb roved lazily over her nipple. "This?"

Her blood was heating. Collecting. "Waking up with a man," she admitted.

His hand left her breast. Slid along her side, her waist. Cupped her hip. He hadn't seemed to notice the scars there the night before.

"Are you sore?" He wasn't referring to the long-healed ridges his fingers slowly traced.

"Are you?" she challenged, if only to pretend she wasn't mortified.

His chest moved against her back and she realized he was chuckling, soundlessly. "Cage—"

"Shh. Relax." He pulled her hair aside and kissed her shoulder. Slid his hand along her thigh. Lulling. Drugging. Then his hand was between her thighs. And he sighed, a sound of such deeply basic appreciation that she melted even more. He kissed her shoulder again. "I want you. Every night. Every morning."

She was swimming in pleasure.

"Marry me, Belle."

She couldn't have heard right. "What?"

Then he moved again, pushing her leg forward just enough to find, to take. Sinking himself into her so smoothly, so sweetly and gently that he stole her heart all over again.

"Oh, yeah," he murmured. "This way. Every way. Marry me."

She arched against him, taking him even deeper.

Twisted her head, looking up at him. "You can't mean it." It was supposed to be women who got their emotions all tangled up with sex. Love. It was happening to her, for pity's sake. It wasn't supposed to happen to him.

But it was.

And his eyes were dead serious. Passion pulled at him, she could see it. Feel it. But he was…serious.

"I want all your mornings," he said evenly. "All your nights. Say yes." He covered her mouth with his and her heart simply cracked wide.

"Yes," she breathed into him.

His arms surrounded her, holding her tight as he rocked into her.

It felt as if he'd rocked right into her soul.

They showered separately. Not because either necessarily wanted to, but because he did need to collect Lucy and get back to the Lazy-B, not spend another endless session drowning in Belle.

There would be plenty of time for that, later.

Much as Belle would have preferred to sit beside him on the long drive, her hand pressing against his leg as if to remind herself of all that had occurred suddenly and not so suddenly, practicality managed to assert itself and having her own vehicle at her disposal was only sensible.

And it gave her more time to pack a real suitcase. To let…everything…sink in a little more.

Cage Buchanan wanted to marry her. And she'd agreed.

When she arrived at the house, Cage wasn't in sight. But Strudel greeted her, barking and dancing around, and Belle hugged the dog, feeling as thoroughly and utterly content with the world as the dog. She lugged her suitcase in through the front door. Cage wanted to tell Lucy their plans together, so she knew he wouldn't have shared the news yet.

But there was no sign of Lucy in the house, either.

She lugged the suitcase up the stairs. Debated briefly where to unpack it. Settled on the guest room since she didn't really have the nerve yet to make herself at home in Cage's room.

She'd never even been *in* Cage's room. So after she'd quickly unpacked, she went in. Smiled a little at the hasty way he'd made his bed. Couldn't very well lecture his daughter about the habit if he didn't try to make his own, could he?

She walked over and picked up the photo beside the bed.

Lucy. Wearing a fancy little ballet tutu, in mid-pirouette. Her limbs strong and true, her face beaming.

Belle set the photo back in its place and went downstairs. Maybe the barn. She'd barely stepped out of the back door before realizing there was a car parked behind the house. A Porsche covered with a fine mist of dust. She eyed it and headed toward the barn.

She hadn't made it halfway when she heard Cage's raised voice, so angry it made the hair on the back of her neck stand up. "She'll have a mother!"

Belle quickened her steps only to stop outside the barn at the sound of her own name.

"Who? Belle Day? Come on, Cage. You really think you can pull that off?"

"She'll marry me."

A ring of amused, female laughter shattered over

Belle. "So you'll finally have some revenge. Gus Day drives your parents off a road and finagles out of any sort of financial settlement, but now you're going to marry his daughter and have your hands on his money through her. And those rancher people, too. The Double-whatever. I'm told they are *very* well off. Not like my parents, of course, but—"

"Is that true?" Belle stepped around the corner of the barn to see Cage squared off with the woman from the pizzeria. He looked as if he'd been pulled backward through a knothole. In contrast, the woman looked perfect. From the top of her gilded head to the toes of her white leather boots.

And they both turned and looked at her when her tennis shoes skidded a little on the hard-packed ground.

Her eyes were green, Belle thought dully. And her face was Lucy's. Why hadn't she noticed that before? "Is that why you proposed?"

Cage's filthy mood at finding Sandi in the barn with Luce when he'd ridden back in after battling with a bawling cow and barbed wire went even farther south. He'd rather battle a mile of barbed wire than have to deal with this moment.

Belle eyeing him, clearly waiting some explanation. Some *something.* "No," he assured flatly.

"Of course it is," Sandi said clucking, her voice dripping kindness. "You swore on your father's grave, remember? Told me all about it," she said to Belle. "How one day he would make the Days hurt as badly as the Buchanans had been." She looked back again at Cage. "Too bad your success doesn't really matter since Lucy's going to be living in Chicago with my parents.

Talk about the original rock and a hard place, right, Cage? Which one to let go of. The ranch or the kid."

He was grateful that Lucy was still out of earshot in the stable where he'd sent her to feed the horses as he rounded on Sandi. "Get…off…my…land." His voice was deadly.

Finally, Sandi had the sense to back off. Her sense of self-preservation kicking in, no doubt because he was two inches shy of dragging her off his property by the roots of her hair and he didn't much care if he broke her neck along the way or not.

She strode toward the barn door. "Good luck with him, honey," she advised Belle. "You're going to need it. If you're smart, you'll rethink the whole marital-bliss thing. My parents will drive him up to his ears in hock if he's not there already, then walk away with Lucy as the prize when they're finished with him." She slid a key chain out of her white purse and jangled the keys. "Of course. He'll have a Day around to finally give him his due." Dust puffed a little around her high heels as she strode out of the barn.

Moments later, her car shot past, gravel and dust spewing from beneath the tires.

Belle was staring at him, her eyes wide. Wounded.

He raked his hands through his hair. He smelled like just what he was. A guy who'd been rolling in mud and manure. Dammit all to hell and back again. Their first day under his roof—together—wasn't supposed to be like this.

Sandi was supposed to be rotting somewhere and he was supposed to be able to pick his time to tell Belle about his legal hassle with the Oldhams and not send her running.

"You could have told me who she was."

"She doesn't matter."

"Of *course* she matters! She's Lucy's mother."

"I didn't think she'd have the nerve to come out here."

Belle's eyes narrowed. "Well she did. This is what all that correspondence with the attorney is about?"

"Yes."

Her chin trembled but she collected herself. "How bad is it? Really?"

"Bad."

"And you need money."

"Yes." The word nearly choked him.

"So." Her knuckles were white. "Everything... Sandi—Lucy's mother—"

"Stop calling her that."

"It's true, though. Along with everything she said. It's all true."

His hands curled, impotence raging through him. "No."

"And I really played right into your hands, didn't I?"

He reached her in two steps, grabbed her arms. "It *wasn't* like that."

"Oh?" She was pale. "Then you're going to tell me that you proposed to me because you *love* me? I should have known better. Realized that there was no way you could have changed so much in these weeks, these last few days. Stupid me." She shrugged out of his hold and ran out of the barn, heading toward the house.

He practically tore the screen off its hinges going after her. Followed her up the stairs and into the guest room. She was shoveling stuff into her suitcase.

He grabbed a handful of sports bras and threw them back out onto the bed. "What I feel for you has been coming on for longer than these past few days and you damn well know it. You're not going to leave like this."

"Really? Do you think you can stop me?"

"I love you, dammit!"

Her hands paused. Shook. Then she scooped the contents out of a drawer and tossed them in the suitcase, her motions stiff. Jerky. "And you never once thought, well, hey, I can make use of this woman? Never, not once?" She waited a long beat. "I didn't think so."

Was he damned forever? He grabbed her shoulders. "It was before I knew you. Really knew you."

"And what about my family? What about if we did—" She broke off, her face a struggle. "If I married you. Then what? You're going to accept my mother? My sister? We're all *Days*. They're my family and they're as important to me as yours is to you."

"Jesus Christ, Belle. The past is the past. I know that. And you're in need of leaving it behind as bad as I am."

"Maybe, I am," she agreed.

"Then we can make a new family. Together. Nothing's changed!"

She stepped away from him, her expression closing. "Everything's changed." She flipped the suitcase closed, despite the edges of shorts, shirts hanging out, and dragged it off the bed. "And just to clear things up. I have *no* money to speak of. When my dad died, my mom had to work just like a million other people to keep a roof over our heads. I went to college on scholarships, not on trust funds. *I* work because I need a paycheck. So, I guess I wouldn't be all that useful to you, after all." She walked out of the room. Thumped her way down the stairs.

His hands fisted. He glared at his old iron-framed bed. Kicked it.

It groaned.

He caught up to Belle before she reached her car. "You love me. Need me. You meant those words, Belle. I know you did."

She threw the suitcase into the passenger seat. It bounced open, spewing its contents. "I'll get over it," she promised thickly, and yanked open the car door, sinking down behind the wheel only to stare at it, mute frustration screaming from her. Her palms slapped the steering wheel and he realized she didn't have the keys.

He blocked her from opening the car door simply by planting himself there. She'd have to climb over the mess of clothes or him to get away. "Don't leave me."

Her head tossed, hair rippling. "Why? Because of Lucy?"

"Because of me."

Her mouth parted. She shook her head. "I don't believe you."

"Goddammit, Belle—"

"Ohmigod." She grabbed the top of the windshield and hoisted herself up in the seat. "Cage. Lucy—"

He caught a blur of motion, the moment seeming to turn to stone in his head. Turning to see what put the horrified expression on Belle's face. Lucy on Satin's back. Struggling to keep him reined in.

He swore and raced out ahead of the horse, aiming

straight at him. In some distant part of his mind he heard Belle scream. Maybe it was the horse.

Maybe it was Lucy who was falling, falling. All over again, even before he could get close enough to snag the beast's reins and drag him under control.

Belle scrambled past him, reaching Lucy first. She huddled on the ground, her hands carefully, gently running over his baby. He fell to his knees beside them.

Satin raced off, hell-bent for leather.

Lucy's eyes were open, tears streaking her face. She tried to move and cried out, clutching her leg and Belle hoarsely ordered her to be still.

His daughter glared at him, her face set in rigid lines. "I heard you guys yelling in the barn. You're sending me away to live with them, aren't you? Just like my mother said."

"No. I won't let it happen."

"She told me she was here for my birthday. That she tried to get here the other day, but she was stuck in an airport in France. But that wasn't it at all, was it?"

He shook his head, wishing he'd been smarter, wishing a million things, all of them too late. "I'm sorry, Lucy."

She angled her eyes over at Belle. "Were you really gonna marry my dad?"

Belle didn't answer that. She looked at Cage, but didn't look at him, and it was worse now than it had ever been in the beginning. "I'm calling Sawyer. We need to get her to the hospital but I don't think we should move her." She touched Lucy's hair gently, then pushed to her feet, running like the wind toward the house.

Lucy closed her eyes. A sprinkle of freckles on her

nose stood out, stark against her white face. "I don't wanna be a dancer, Dad. I don't wanna be anything like my mother."

He folded her hand in his. "You will dance," he said roughly, "and you will ride and do all the things you love, and you have *never* been like her. And I'm not letting you go anywhere you don't want to go. Clear?"

She started to nod, groaned.

Belle returned, blankets in her arms. "The medivac's on its way. Twenty minutes, max." She knelt next to Lucy, spreading the blankets over her. Held up her fingers for Lucy to count, making comforting noises.

Then the chopper arrived, settling out in the field. Same place as it had done seven months earlier. Only then, it had landed on a skiff of snow.

Cage and Belle ran alongside the stretcher they quickly loaded Lucy on. He ducked low, avoiding the blades that had barely stopped rotating. Belle hung back, already moving away from the clearing. She didn't need to be told there was a premium of space inside the helicopter.

One of the techs was telling Cage to finish fastening his safety harness. He did so, watching out the side as the helicopter lifted. The wind whipped Belle's hair in a frenzy around her shoulders as they left her behind.

As far as hospitals went, Weaver's was pretty small. Cage had paced from one end of the building to the other about a million times over before Dr. Rebecca Clay finally reappeared after closing herself with his daughter behind a series of doors some bull of a woman in starched whites had dared him to cross.

The slender brunette held an oversize folder in her hands and he knew from experience they contained the X rays Lucy had just received.

The doctor smiled at him and gestured at the row of hard plastic chairs lining a sun-filled waiting room. "Let's sit," she encouraged. "Lucy's doing pretty well. No signs of concussion. I want to keep her awhile just to be cautious. A few days."

He stared, waiting for the big *but*. "What about her leg?"

Rebecca sighed a little. "There are no fractures, which is a good thing. We've immobilized it for now. But she has done some damage. How extensive, I couldn't tell you. She'll need to see her orthopedist. I know you have a perfectly fine one, but George Valenzuela from the Huffington Clinic has agreed to come up and consult, if you'd like. Belle called him while you and Lucy were on your way in. He specializes in pediatric cases. But you don't have to decide anything right now. We've given Lucy something for the pain." She patted his hand. "They're getting her settled in a room. I'll have someone take you to her."

He nodded. An hour later, he was sitting beside his daughter's hospital bed. She was sound asleep, her leg back in a brace similar to the one she'd worn for so many weeks after her first round of surgery.

He called his house but there was no answer. Called a dozen times throughout the night. His house. Belle's house. The cell phone she avoided as often as not.

By morning he faced it.

Belle was gone.

But if she thought things were over between them, she didn't know him as well as he'd thought.

Chapter Seventeen

Cage eyed the row of men. And women. When he'd driven up the circular driveway of the Double-C Ranch, they'd all turned to watch, seeming to form a line. A significant line looking incongruous against the backdrop of colorful balloons tied by ribbons to nearly every stationary object.

"They don't look real happy to see us." Lucy's voice was subdued.

He hadn't figured showing up this way would be easy. "They invited you weeks ago to Angel's birthday party. It's not you they're not happy to see," he assured her. And, he reminded himself, Belle had visited Lucy each of the three days she'd been in the hospital. Avoided him like the plague, true, but she'd come all the same.

The driveway was congested with dozens of vehicles, not all belonging to the various members of the Clay family, he figured. Their reputation for throwing a celebration was well known, and it wouldn't have surprised Cage to count nearly half the population of Weaver as present.

It was the first time Cage had ever been to the Double-C Ranch, though. For any reason.

He didn't bother with trying to find an open place to park. There were none, so he just stopped his truck close enough where Lucy wouldn't have to drag her brace around any farther than necessary.

Even though there was music riding the air, right alongside the distinct smell of grilling meat that would've made his mouth water if it hadn't already been filled with crow, it still seemed as if a silence settled over the throng as he and Lucy slowly crossed an oval stretch of green grass toward that line of people.

"I don't see Belle." Lucy muttered an aside, looking worried.

Neither did Cage.

"Hey, Lucy." Ryan Clay grinned, seemingly unaware of the collective stares of his parents—Sawyer and Rebecca—aunts, uncles and grandparents as he walked into view, a plate in his hand on which a tower of food wavered dangerously. At sixteen, he was the oldest of Belle's nieces and nephews and the brown-haired kid with his father's blue eyes seemed to take the role with due seriousness. "Nice hardware you got on your leg there. Does it come off? 'Cause some of us're heading out to the swimming hole in a while and we wouldn't want you to sink." He jerked his head, assuming that she'd follow.

Lucy cast a look up at Cage. "Go ahead."

She needed no second urging and slowly worked her way toward Ryan.

Which left Cage facing that line of people alone.

He focused on the slender, auburn-haired woman who stood at the center. Gloria Day. Gloria *Clay*. And of all the men there, eyeing him with various degrees of warning, it was facing her that struck him the hardest. He walked closer. Until he could see the strands of silver in her auburn hair and the gentle lines beside her eyes that were the same shape and size as her daughter's, if a different color. They were the lines of a woman who'd done a lot of smiling in her life.

Definitely not in evidence now.

"If you've come to bring your daughter to celebrate with us, you're welcome," she said after a moment. "But if you've come to cause my girl more heartache, you can turn right on your heel and go."

"Give the boy a chance to talk, Gloria." Squire stood beside his wife and Cage could see the speculation in the man's squinty gaze before he turned his focus back to the fat wedge of cake on the plate he held.

Cage pulled off his hat and got to it. "I've nursed a grudge for a long time, Mrs.— " get it right "—Clay. Way back, it was sometimes the only thing that got me through another day." He figured he imagined the speck of sympathy in her eyes before her lashes swept down. "And I'm willing to admit that I managed to make a comfortable habit out of blaming your late husband for things. When you married Squire and moved up to Weaver—well, I let it bug me more than I should have. And I'm sorry for that. For a lot of things."

"I don't need your apology, Cage." Gloria looked up at him. "Nor do you need mine. What happened all those years ago was a tragedy. So, if that's all you came to say, then—"

"It isn't." A lifetime of fending for himself, on his own, struggling to keep what was his clawed at him. "I'm in love with your daughter, Mrs. Clay. And it's the first time I've ever *been* in love. The kind of love that matters. The kind that'll last a person their whole life if they're smart. And up to now, I've pretty much made a mess of it. I know I'm a stubborn man."

"He's right," Squire put in conversationally. "Cussed stubborn. I've offered plenty for that pretty piece of property he's got many a time and it took him until—"

"Squire," Gloria chided. "Hush up."

"What?" He looked around, innocence personified, which nobody bought because Squire Clay's craftiness was too well known. "I'm only agreeing with the boy. He's stubborn." He lifted his fork and pointed before stabbing it into his cake. "But he's got gumption, too. I'll give him that."

Damned if Cage didn't feel his neck getting hot. He'd had a meeting or two with the man over the past few days. But he hadn't bared any more thoughts than necessary and he hadn't said squat about Belle. It wasn't Squire he needed to get square with.

It was Gloria. "And I'm proud," Cage went on, determined to get through this even if it killed him.

"Too proud, I'd say."

He jerked, the sound of Belle's voice ripping a layer of skin off his soul. He turned and there she stood in a skinny red top and narrow black jeans. Want slammed hard in his chest and it had nothing to do with the physical.

"You cut your hair."

Her hands flew to the shoulder-length strands as if she wanted to hide that glaring fact. Then she straightened and lifted her chin. "So?"

She'd done it because of him. There was no doubt inside him. And it hurt. Not because he cared if she had long hair or short hair or no hair. But because he knew what she'd been trying to do. Amputate the memory of them by lopping off her hair.

He set his shoulders, his fingers digging into his hat. "I'm *too* proud," he continued evenly. If Belle wanted him to crawl, he'd crawl, but damned if he was gonna enjoy the process.

"And stubborn," she said, crossing her arms, staring down her nose.

He gave her a sideways look. "I believe that's ground I've covered already."

She sniffed and looked away. But her high-and-mighty act was just that. Because he'd seen her eyes. Looking wet and bruised as pansies after a hard rain. Knowing he'd put that look there made him ache inside.

Gloria lifted her hand, sighing a little. "Stop." She stepped forward, breaking the ranks, and continued until she looked right up in Cage's face. "How is your mother?"

It ought to have ripped, that question. And maybe it would have just a few weeks earlier. "She's doing well. Thank you," he tacked on.

"I'm glad. My husband would have been glad. He worried about you and her a lot. He tried to speak with you, more than once, to tell you how sorry he was. But he was also deeply concerned about intruding on your grief."

He hadn't imagined the sympathy in Gloria's eyes, he realized. But along with that was also a vein of steel. He was a parent, too, and he could respect that. He'd messed with her daughter. "I appreciate knowing that."

"He tried to help, financially. The money you thought came from your parents' insurance came from him."

Belle's *"What?"* was an echo of his own.

"I know it wasn't much," Gloria went on. "Not enough to have lasted out all these years for your mother's care. You've done that. On your own, I'm sure. Doing a fine job of it."

"Why are you telling us this now?" Belle stopped beside him, facing her mother. "Why, after all these years?"

"Because I think—" Gloria's eyes were thoughtful "—Cage is ready to accept the truth of it, now. Aren't you?"

He remembered the day the check had come from the insurance. "I fought the insurance company for months," he said. "Trying to get them to settle. They claimed my father'd let the policy lapse. Then I later got a letter. And a check. Saying they'd been in error." The lawyer he'd hired had finally come through. Cage had always figured the guy had kept on the case only so he could collect his contingency fee.

That money had done a lot of things, not least of which was getting Sandi Oldham on that plane to Brazil and out of his life. "The insurance company wasn't making up for an error, like I was told," he concluded swallowing down hard on that. It wasn't an easy pill.

Gloria shook her head. "Given your situation, and what he learned about you, Gus believed that you'd never have accepted the money outright from him. He knew that the only thing you wanted was for your parents to still be with you. And that was something he couldn't accomplish. No matter how much he wished otherwise. I never was sure it was the right way to handle it, but it was Gus's decision and there was no moving that man when he'd set his mind on something." Her lips curved a little. "I know a little bit about dealing with stubborn men," she added.

And the man's actions hadn't left much over for his own family when he'd died not three years later, Cage figured.

"I'm sorry." He was.

Her hand brushed down his arm in a soothing motion. "There's no need to be," she said quietly. Then she stepped back, folding her arms across her chest. Squire was there and she leaned against him. "Not about that, anyway," she said. Her gaze encompassed him and Belle. And he knew that Gloria already knew some of what he'd come to say. He doubted there were many secrets, if any, that were kept between herself and Squire.

He looked down at Belle. "I'm selling the Lazy-B."

Belle sucked in a breath as Cage's words penetrated the glaze she'd been dwelling in for days. "What? Why? To who?"

"Because it's time," he said.

Her eyes burned way deep down in their sockets. "You shouldn't have to sell the Lazy-B, Cage. It's your home. There must be another way to fight against the Oldham's suit."

"I'm not selling 'cause of them. I'm moving Lucy to Cheyenne."

She wrapped her arms around her middle, glancing over at the girl who was sitting in a lawn chair some-one had given up for her, a hot dog in her hand that held nowhere near the interest that watching *them* did. "Have you *told* her that?"

His lips tightened a little. "Don't you want to know why?"

"No," she lied. "Have some food. There's plenty. If you can stand to eat anything touched by a *Day's* hands."

"Annabelle!" Gloria stared at her.

Belle's eyes flooded. Seemed they weren't eternally dry after all even though they ought to have been given the number of times she'd bawled over the past week. And she was making a scene, just exactly what Cage had to hate most of all, airing his personal matters in public.

Particularly *this* public.

"Don't worry, Mrs. Clay," Cage said evenly. "She's not saying anything I haven't thought at one time or an-other." His jaw slanted. Centered. "And I'm sorry for that, too."

Belle pressed her hands to her temples. "Maybe we should talk about this somewhere else."

"No," Cage said, shocking her silent. "Right here will do. I'm in love with you, Belle Day. I proposed to you once, but I'll keep doing it until you realize I'm not giving up on you. On us. You think I can't handle being a part of your family. Well, I'm here. And I'm not going anywhere until you can start believing otherwise."

She dropped her hands. Stared at him. All conversation had ceased. They could have heard the grass growing if they listened.

"I'm a simple man, Belle. And I don't have a lot." He made a wry sound, nearly soundless. "I've got... baggage." He looked over at his daughter and smiled a little. "And I'm not talking about that one, there, 'cause she's definitely the best thing I have going for me. Which I guess you know better than most. I've spent nearly my whole life fending for myself and opening up about it isn't my forte."

Belle gnawed the inside of her cheek as Cage stepped closer to her. His black shirt rippled in a sudden flutter of wind that tugged the tablecloths and dragged at the balloons.

"We can't change the past," he said. "It shapes us, but it doesn't have to define us. Luce and I are going to Cheyenne because that's where *you're* going."

"Says who?" she challenged thickly.

"That doctor you arranged to come up and consult on Lucy's case. Dr. Valenzuela. He said you're the best physical therapist Huffington's got and was mighty glad you were finally going to be back on staff."

"Well, gee." Her tone was stiff enough to hold up barbed wire. "Thanks for the validation."

"Is this a battle over *your* pride, then?" he asked. "Yes, Lucy can be treated at Huffington. But we're going to Cheyenne because of *you* and it doesn't have jack to do with your job, so get off your bloody high horse!"

She glared at him. "I'm interfering. I'm nosy. I'm riding high horses. What on earth could you possibly want with me, then?"

"God only knows," he said tightly, "because you're a pain in my heart like you would not believe. I married a woman when I was seventeen years old, but she was *never* part of my family. She was never my wife in any sense of the word. You're the only one I've ever asked to be, and you throw it in my face."

"You only proposed because you—" She barely managed to bite back the words. He'd proposed while they'd been making love.

"Because I wanted to spend my next fifty years loving you? Making a home with you?" His voice was rising furiously. "Giving Lucy a brother or a sister maybe? Watching them grow up with your brown eyes and your laughter? Yes, I should have told you about the custody suit. But it didn't have squat to do with my loving you and it still doesn't! Now are you going to marry me, or not? And don't be looking around for everyone's opinion, here. Because this is not between us and them, it's you and me, Belle."

She was shaking. "Could have fooled me," she whispered, "considering the way you're announcing it to all the world, here."

His eyebrows drew together. His tone gentled. He took another step nearer. "You want me on bended knee with all these witnesses to beg? Will that convince you?" He started to go down.

She shook her head and grabbed his arms, staying him. "I've never wanted you to beg," she whispered. "I just wanted you to love me."

"You have that, Belle." He slid his fingers through her hair, drawing it away from her face. "I've worked out this stuff with the Oldhams," he said quietly. "They took Satin back where he belongs."

"But…how? When? Isn't Lucy upset?"

"When you were hiding from me around hospital walls, and not answering your phone no matter what time I called," he murmured. "When it seemed I had to prove my feelings for you didn't have anything to do with anyone other than you. I did exactly what my attorney advised me not to do, and called them myself. And no. Lucy isn't upset. Now that the horse is gone she's stopped pretending she wasn't scared spitless of it. She thought she needed to be ready to ride, but she wasn't. When she is, when her leg is better, it might take a while to get her back in the saddle, but she'll get there with a horse she's not already afraid of."

She could hardly draw breath. "And what about the Oldhams?"

"I should have done it a long time ago. But there's that stubbornness of mine at work again, trying to prove I can do anything and everything better than everyone else. They never wanted complete custody of Lucy. They just wanted to have the grandchild Sandi'd been denying them."

"And you believed them?"

"I did once they faxed me confirmation they'd dropped the suit. Came this morning." He patted his pocket. Pulled out a piece of paper and showed it to her. "If I hadn't been so stuck on pride and just let them visit when they asked, none of this would have happened. The gifts they sent. The horse." He shook his head. "But then we wouldn't have had a reason for *you*." His voice went a little hoarse at that and he cleared his throat. "In exchange, they can come and visit Lucy *at* the Lazy-B and she doesn't have to sneak phone calls to them, anymore."

"Oh, Cage." She could see the relief in his eyes as he slid the notice back in his pocket. Knew how deep the relief ran. "It was that simple?"

"Well." His lips twisted a little, and she knew then that it hadn't been quite so simple. "In this case it's the end result that matters," he said. "So you see. I'm here strictly on my own. No agendas. Nothing. Maybe nothing is the word you need to focus on, though. I've got some prospects once I finish the sale of my place and get my neck out of debt. It won't be like running my own spread, but I—"

"We," she corrected huskily, catching his hand in hers, pressing it against her face. "We, not I, Cage. That's what families are about, aren't they?"

"We," he repeated slowly, as if he were testing the taste of it. The weight of it. "I guess they are. So is this a yes, Miss Belle Day? No changing your mind, no turning back. Will you marry me?"

She nodded. A tear slid past her lashes and his thumb caught it.

"Mrs. Clay?" He raised his voice, never taking his vivid gaze off Belle's face. "Do I have permission to marry your daughter, or not?"

"I guess you'd better," Gloria said faintly. "Or we might have a revolt on our hands."

Belle slowly looked past Cage's wide shoulders to see a horde of expectant faces. Her mother. Her sister.

And then there was Lucy, who looked ready to vibrate right out of her shoes.

"Welcome to the family, son," Squire said blandly.

Cage's lips tilted and his eyes met hers. "I love you, Belle."

"I love you, too, Cage."

"So hurry up and kiss her already, 'cause I want to go to the swimming hole with Ryan and his friends," Lucy said loudly.

"She has kind of a smart mouth sometimes," Cage murmured. "Don't let it scare you off."

"Not in this lifetime," Belle promised.

"Now," Squire said. "About the ranch. Some details we gotta—"

"Hush up, Squire," Gloria chided.

He grunted.

"Don't let them scare you off," Belle whispered back.

His hands held a fine tremble as he cupped her face in them. His eyes gleamed. "Not in this lifetime," he promised.

And at last, Belle believed him.

Then he wrapped his arms around her and kissed her.

And neither one heard anything further.

Epilogue

"Howard. Gorgon. Beowulf." Belle kept her voice low and watched Cage's lips turn up at the corners. Three months had passed since the day he'd shown up at the Double-C. Three months during which she found every opportunity to make him smile. She loved that smile.

She loved him. And each day that passed, she loved him more.

"Unique," he whispered easily, shifting in the folding chair. He looked over his shoulder, but there was still no sign of the bride and groom. "I hope our wedding doesn't last this long," he murmured. "I should have brought a book to read or something."

She contained a laugh. "You've been friends with Emmy Johannson for a long time. You *should* be here for her wedding. She and Larry are probably getting some pictures taken. They'll be here soon enough. Here. You can finish my punch." She nudged her cup toward him.

He took it. Drank it down. Even though he seemed calm, she knew he wasn't entirely comfortable. Emmy and Larry's wedding wasn't as large as theirs was shaping up to be, but it *was* well-attended. Since he'd proposed, he'd been a more frequent sight in Weaver, but this was the first time they'd attended such a thoroughly social event.

"Come on," she wheedled, tilting her head a little. Sliding her fingers inside the cuff of his handsome gray suit. "We'll be married soon ourselves and you *still* won't tell me your real first name. Don't you think you're taking things a little far? When we pick up the wedding license I'm going to find out, you know."

He caught her exploring hand, lifted it and kissed her knuckles. "I never kept it secret from you, Belle."

She sniffed, but they both knew it was more for effect than anything else. Then Hope—who was a teacher like Larry was—and Tristan rejoined the table. They'd been dancing.

Hope let out a breathy laugh. Her pregnancy barely showed yet, but she was the picture of health from her toffee-colored long hair to her gleaming violet eyes. "Lucy must have worked really hard to be ready for today without needing her crutches. She and Anya look so pretty in their bridesmaid dresses."

"Too grown-up if you ask me," Cage murmured, looking over to where his daughter stood. Lucy and Anya— dressed in matching long red velvet gowns—were surrounded by friends. Many of them male. He looked over to Tristan. He and Hope already had a five-year-old son. "If you two have a girl, you'll know what I mean."

Tristan grinned. His fingers looped through his wife's. "I've got nieces," he said. "So I already have an idea." He looked at Cage. "How's it feel to be partners with Squire?"

"He takes some watching." Cage looked amused. "He's got Double-C hooves grazing on Lazy-B land now."

"You'll buy him back out again," Belle assured. Knowing that Cage one day would. He was simply too proud not to. She understood that now. Understood so much about the boy he'd never really been allowed to be. And she was eternally grateful that he hadn't sold the Lazy-B outright. Not even to her stepfather who was currently circling the dance floor with her mother.

A commotion near the door of the church hall brought their attention around. Emmy and Larry had arrived. They didn't form a traditional receiving line, but went around to greet their guests in their seats. When the couple reached their table, Cage stood and gruffly bussed Emmy on the cheek and shook Larry's hand. "Congratulations."

Emmy beamed at Belle. "I know *you're* the one to get Cage here. Thanks."

"He wouldn't have missed Lucy being a bridesmaid," Belle assured. And Emmy had been one of the few people in Weaver he'd peripherally let into his life in the first place. It may have been more of necessity than anything else since she'd helped so much with Lucy over the years, but she knew he was happy for Emmy and Larry.

"Anya's so excited about going to New York with Lucy and the Oldhams next summer. I don't know which thrills her more. Seeing a Broadway show, or riding on the plane there." Emmy squeezed Cage's hand briefly. "Thanks for including her."

"Thanks for letting her go."

She smiled happily and with Larry's arm around her, they moved on to the next table.

Belle leaned toward Cage. "You've known Emmy since you were kids. Does *she* know your real name?"

The DJ had switched tempos and a slow sexy tune wailed from the speakers, heavy on sax and bass. Cage held out his hand for her. "You know my real name. Come on. I know you want to dance."

She did. But she'd been content to stay by Cage, believing he'd have no interest in it. She put her hand in his and he took her into the center of the swaying couples, ignoring the surprised looks they received. Then he pulled her into his arms. Two seconds later, she knew he wasn't just a shuffle-your-feet dancer. He knew how to dance. Properly.

"Don't look so surprised," he said after a moment, his eyes smiling. "My mom made sure I learned a long time ago. Did you think Luce gets her coordination all from Sandi?"

Belle shook her head. "She gets her heart from you," she whispered. And right now, *her* heart felt so full she was afraid it would start leaking out her eyes. "And how would I know your real name? You've only told me it's unique. What am I supposed to—" She broke off, suspicious at the glint of humor in his eyes, and realization finally dawned. "Oh. No. No way."

"It's an old family name," he said gruffly. "And I know it's—"

"Unique," she inserted. "All along, you've told me. Your name is actually *Unique*." She laughed. Pressed her lips together and giggled some more. "Please tell me we don't have to stick with the family name when you and I start having children," she finally managed.

"You don't have to do anything," he assured. "Except let me love you for the rest of my days. You're my life, you know," he whispered softly, for her ears alone.

She twined her arms around his neck and it didn't matter that they were in the middle of someone else's wedding reception. Her heart *did* overflow.

That's just what happened sometimes when a woman found everything she'd ever wanted with one very unique man.

"And you're mine, Cage Buchanan. You're mine."

* * * * *

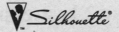

If you enjoyed what you just read,
then we've got an offer you can't resist!

Take 2 bestselling
love stories FREE!
Plus get a FREE surprise gift!

Receive a FREE hardcover book from

H A R L E Q U I N   R O M A N C E®

in September!

**Harlequin Romance celebrates the launch of
the line's new cover design by offering you
this exclusive offer valid only in September,
only in Harlequin Romance.**

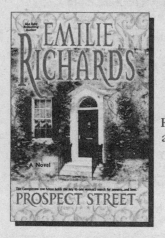

To receive your
FREE HARDCOVER BOOK
written by bestselling author
Emilie Richards, send us four
proofs of purchase from any
September 2004 Harlequin
Romance books. Further details
and proofs of purchase can be
found in all September 2004
Harlequin Romance books.

*Must be postmarked
no later than October 31.*

**Don't forget to be one of the first
to pick up a copy of the new-look
Harlequin Romance novels in September!**

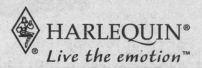

HARLEQUIN®
Live the emotion™

Visit us at www.eHarlequin.com

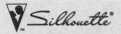

COMING NEXT MONTH

#1639 MARRYING MOLLY—Christine Rimmer
Bravo Family Ties
Salon owner Molly O'Dare vowed to never be single *and* pregnant.
That is, until a passionate love affair landed her in both of these
categories. The child's father—wealthy and dashingly handsome
Tate Bravo—insisted on marrying Molly. But she was determined to
resist until he could offer exactly what she wanted: true love.

#1640 THE PRINCE'S BRIDE—Lois Faye Dyer
The Parks Empire
Wedding planner Emily Parks had long since given up her dream
of starting a family and decided to focus on her career. She never
imagined that the dashing Prince Lazhar Eban would ever want
her to be his bride, but little did she know that what began as a
business proposition would turn into the marriage proposal she'd
always dreamed of!

#1641 THE DEVIL YOU KNOW—Laurie Paige
Seven Devils
When Roni Dalton literally fell onto FBI agent Adam Smith's table
at a restaurant, she set off a chain of mutual passion that neither
could resist. Adam claimed that he was too busy to get involved, but
when he suddenly succumbed to their mutual attraction, Roni was
determined to change this self-proclaimed singleton into a
marriage-minded man.

#1642 NANNY IN HIDING—Patricia Kay
The Hathaways of Morgan Creek
On the run from her evil ex-husband, Amy Jordan accepted blue-
eyed Bryce Hathaway's offer to be his children's nanny. This
wealthy single dad was immediately intrigued by the beautiful
runaway, but if he discovered that this caring, gentle woman was
actually a nanny *in hiding,* would he be help her out—or turn her in?

#1643 WRONG TWIN, RIGHT MAN—Laurie Campbell
Beth Montoya and her husband, Rafael, were on the verge of
divorce when Beth barely survived a brutal train accident. When she
was struck with amnesia and mistakenly identified as her
twin sister, Anne, Rafael offered to take care of "Anne" while she
recovered. Suddenly lost passion flared between them…but then her
true identity started to surface.…

#1644 MAKING BABIES—Wendy Warren
Recently divorced Elaine Lowry yearned for a baby of her own.
Enter Mitch Ryder—sinfully handsome and looking for an heir to
carry on his family name. He insisted that their marriage be strictly
business, but what would happen if she couldn't hold up her end of
the deal?